1 MONTH OF
FREE
READING

at
www.ForgottenBooks.com

By purchasing this book you are eligible for one month membership to ForgottenBooks.com, giving you unlimited access to our entire collection of over 1,000,000 titles via our web site and mobile apps.

To claim your free month visit:

www.forgottenbooks.com/free179512

ISBN 978-0-484-61575-4
PIBN 10179512

The Home-Story Series.

STORIES FOR LEISURE HOURS.

By AUGUSTA LARNED.

THREE ILLUSTRATIONS.

————◆◆◆————

NEW YORK:

NELSON & PHILLIPS.

CINCINNATI: HITCHCOCK & WALDEN.

SUNDAY-SCHOOL DEPARTMENT.

CONTENTS.

Illustrations.

STORIES FOR LEISURE HOURS.

THE PROFESSIONAL BABY.

IF MARY MALONY had hung out a sign from the fourth story front window of the tenement house in Cork Alley, where she lived, saying, " Baby to let or lend," the fact that she had such a convenient piece of property on hand could not have been better understood throughout the neighborhood than it already was.

The baby, God bless its dear, bright eyes! was not one of Mary Malony's own brood. None of her frowzy, freckled young tatterdemalions would have answered the purpose for which babies are made professional.

This particular mite of humanity was the *ne plus ultra* of good children. It early developed a remarkable genius for being " turned off," lying in clothes baskets, and reposing contentedly upon dresser shelves. Altogether, it was a winsome, dimpled, happy creature, that every body loved. I do believe this baby would have flourished all the same hanging on a peg, it made such unseemly sport, considering its size, of the trials and troubles of this great, big world.

Its mother had been a char-woman in a vast down-town building, all honeycombed with offices. Once she slipped and fell on the main stairway with a bucket of boiling suds, and between the scalds and bruises and some internal hurt that day received she never did a stroke of work afterward.

When she died Mary Malony took her baby, because "them two"—Mary and the mother that was gone, "rest her sowl!"—had scrubbed together a deal in their time; and, being the "owldest and bist friends of each other's, had quarreled and fit a deal too. God forgive her! he knew how quick teched she was." Besides this, it was pure charity. The purest article of that kind hides in just such dingy, ill-smelling rooms as Mary Malony's.

The baby's father proved excellent food for powder and ball. He was shot in the war—one of those dumb, nameless ones that make so many pathetic little hummocks on Southern battle-fields. As for Dennis Malony, Mary's male incumbrance, he was substantially what Mary called him, a "poor coot," and guzzled his soul away in dram-shops—never seeking to interfere with the divinity that drudged and toiled, scolded and stormed, up in that fourth-story room, and yet at heart was as mellow and sweet-flavored as an October pippin.

There was the baby, Sophy by name. The dusty old cobbler who hammered all day in the basement, looking as if every part of him had been cut out of the same rusty piece of stuff—clothes not excepted—named her little All-bright; and Mother Spoon, the rag-picker, named her Happy-go-lucky ; and Mr. Sprat, the sentimental young man in the Pharmaceutical and Chemical Hall, otherwise a two-shelf apothecary shop, called her Twinkle, because he said her eyes danced just like stars. And in some way Mr. Sprat's poetical name came into favor, and quite put out all the others.

It would take too much time to tell just how Twinkle became a professional baby. Mary Malony, standing over the washtub, a sort of Hibernian Venus, in a cloud of soapy steam, often tried to excuse away the very best action of her life. But folks might say she was unjust to her own flesh and blood when she took another mouth to fill. Truth to tell, there was always an unoccupied, aching corner in each one of those little Malony stomachs; but they never begrudged any thing shared with Twinkle.

Mary always ended her harangue by a fond glance toward the little fair, sunny creature, looking like a dove strayed off accidentally into a flock of long-legged goslings. "She must scratch for herself as soon as iver she can," would come next, with a half-suppressed sigh, and then rub-a-dub-dub back to the wash-board. The tender age at which the young fry of Cork Alley began "to scratch for themselves" was marvelous.

Polly French (misnamed, because she was really English) observed once that Twinkle would be a treasure to the "profession." Polly was a little in that line herself, she ought to know. They wanted "hinfants" that could stop the public; and folks might as well try to get past that baby's face as past a bunch of violets.

That was the beginning of it. The profession at which Polly hinted appertained to what she *naively* termed the " haskers." There they go asking all day long, through the streets and lanes ; but not always, as the Scripture promises, receiving. There go askers on one leg, and askers on no legs, hopping like toads along the ground ; askers exhibiting every kind of repulsive deformity and pitiable misfortune; askers that lie and thieve ; and others, with pale, pinched faces, who are dying for succor, because their profession is in such evil odor.

Cork Alley was not nearly as professional as Dublin-street, and Dublin-street in that respect could not compare with Backslum Corner. There were, however, plenty of people in Cork Alley ready to strip off the decent clothes given them at some mission school, and send their children out in rags to beg through the streets. God knows they were poor enough ; but nothing can excuse the wicked deception.

Honest Mary Malony, who would scorn to beg as long as she could earn sixpence with her ten fingers, refused the " loan ". of Twinkle to all her neighbors but those in actual want of

food and fire. So, when a shock-headed, smeary-
faced child put her head into Mary's door, with
a "Plaze, could I be afther borry'n Twinkle
to-day?" Mary sighed, and said, "She's an
orphin, as poor as God's birds that hop on the
bough. It's no lie you'll be afther tellin'. But
mind and see no har-rum comes to the darlint
or I'll wallop ye, shure!"

It was always stipulated that a part of the
profit should belong to Twinkle; and the hoard
of dirty pennies, so gathered, at the bottom of
Mary's cracked china vase, were as sacred in
her sight as if they had been blessed by the
Pope.

So Twinkle was carried out, day after day, to
knock with her tiny, unconscious hand at the
heart of the great, hard world.

It was the morning that Tom Malony's "hin"
laid her first egg. I should like to tell you all
about this remarkable fowl if I only had time.
How many story germs lie wrapped up in every
little story-bud! This event was of the greatest
possible importance to the Malonys, great and
small; for sinee the hen first entered the family
various anticipated blessings had been referred
to it.

"Gosh!" said Tom, trying to use a manly native American word, "wont we smell custard when the ole hin begins to lay?"

"Bedad!" exclaimed Kate Malony, turning round, with a knife sticking in a half-peeled potato, "that would be a wicked extravagance. We'll sell the eggs and buy mother a breastpin like Miss Mangel's, shure!"

"Hooray! hooray for mother's breastpin!" shouted all the small fry at the top of their good, strong lungs. There was one promising thing about those ragged young Malonys— they were always prepared to "hooray" for mother.

The counting of the eggs before they were laid went on vigorously. Various nests, in old baskets and boxes, were arranged to make laying both easy and pleasant. The happiest results were anticipated; but it would seem that Tommy and his little brothers and sisters had squeezed all the laying genius out of this unfortunate chicken. As for Twinkle, bless her dear innocence! she only drooled energetically, and laughed as loud as she could when the hen was on exhibition, and that happened to be about all the time, as she was a very accomplished bird, and could do any thing but lay. Speckle's grand one-leg act round a chalk circle, gently urged to what Tommy called "coming up to the scratch" by a thread tied to her foot, the promiscuous rabble of Cork Alley voted almost as exciting as "Dad Macervin's" performing monkey.

A good appetite is considered a great bless-ing. But did you ever think that it is only a blessing to lucky people, like you and me, who don't have to bother their heads about where the next meal is coming from? The huge, overgrown appetites of those little Malonys—so much out of proportion to the size of their bodies—almost worried Mary's life out, and made her days and nights one round of dull, drudging toil. Speckle, the hen, shared this peculiarity with the others, and ate her head off regularly at least three times a day.

When those brilliant hopes of a fortune, based on that obstinate fowl's eggs, began to fade a little from the minds of the less sanguine, Mary, with a dark look, would glance from the uncon-scious Speckle on her favorite perch, Tommy's shoulder, to a little black pot that stood in the corner, and then back to Speckle, as much as to say, "Great gormandizing hens, that can lay and wont lay, must at last come to pot."

Tommy understood the look, and his peace of mind was gone. He made the most touching appeals to his hen's moral sensibilities by quoting the noble example of old Grimes's chicken:

> " And every day she laid two eggs,
>   And Sundays she laid three."

But it failed to move Speckle's stony crop. In desperation, he thought of offering her to Barnum as a highly-trained fowl of immense genius ; although down deep in his brave heart he still believed in her, and held a little glimmering hope that in spite of all Speckle would some day make his fortune. Nights he would often wake up out of some dream of a little Irish boy's paradise, and, nudging his brother Sandy, whisper,

"Sandy, didn't ye hear the old hin a cacklin'?"

But Sandy never heard the ghost of a cackle, or any body else. The great deed was done in secrecy and silence, when least expected.

Speckle chose a very queer place to lay her egg. She dropped it on top of a refuse-barrel

full of worthless traps, that belonged to the
Crow's mother. The Crow herself found it,
and ran with it, while it was yet warm, up to
Tommy.

"O, mother!" cried the boy, half beside himself, as he hopped round like a parched pea,
with one foot in a very holey stocking and
the other bare, and one ragged jacket-sleeve
off and the other on, "the old bid has done
it at last!"

Mary Malony stopped spanking little Pat;
and little Pat, he stopped crying, and began to
shout; and all the others, Twinkle not excepted,
hooted and hooted at such a rate you would
have thought nothing less than a shower of
fairy gold had fallen down the chimney.

Now, I am going to tell you how that very
first egg that Speckle ever laid did bring great
good luck to the Malonys. Many fine, grand fortunes have turned on a pivot no larger than the
little end of a hen's egg.

Quite close to the door, with a meeching,
apologetic air, as if all the stiffening had been
cuffed out of her, stood the Crow. I suppose
the boys had given her that name because she
was such a thin, slinky creature. Her hair

was too limp to snarl, and her old tea-colored dress clung to her legs like the tail of a whipped dog.

"Shure, was you afther findin' it, Lindy?" Mary asked, as pleased as could be, while she patted the pearly shell, holding it affectionately in the hollow of her great red hand.

The girl nodded with a sort of shy, wrinkly smile on her yellow visage. "I found it atop of our old bar'l. I know'd it was yourn, and thought it would plaze ye."

Mary looked surprised and softened. The Crow had a bad name for thieving, and she wondered at this sign of honesty. I am glad to say, right here, that the Crow had a far worse name than she deserved. I am also glad to say that Tom colored under his freckles, and looked as if he wanted to hide behind a cabbage leaf; for he remembered more than one occasion on which he had mocked and jeered at the Crow, along with the rest of the rabble of Cork Alley.

"Hooray for the Crow!" cried Tom, trying to pluck up spirit. "You shall have an egg when the old hen lays three eggs a day." He kicked Sandy slyly on the shin. Sandy was busy releasing a flap from one of the numerous air-holes that ventilated Tom's trowsers.

"I don't ax none of your eggs, Tom Malony." And a little jet of fire danced out of the Crow's dull eyes. "But, ma'am," and her tone changed to one of almost tearful supplication, "if I could take out Twinkle to-day! Sha'n't a mite o' harm come to her; 'deed, there sha'n't!"

Mary had always heretofore refused this girl's applications for Twinkle because she knew no good of her. But the influence of old Speckle's happy effort was like a hot sun on a snow-bank, and she yielded to the Crow's request, partly, I am sure, because she knew the poor creature's mother was sick—from whisky drinking, be it sadly whispered, but nevertheless sick—while the cupboard was empty, and last month's rent overdue.

Now we behold Twinkle wrapped in what Mary called the "flirt" of an old shawl—warmly, securely wrapped by her loving hands; and, after receiving two smothering kisses all round from the little Malonys, carried out in the Crow's bony arms. It seemed as though they were hardly strong enough to support the baby's contented weight; but they clasped the little creature in a hungry way, as if she was the burden for which they had long been aching.

There was no need of the Crow's trying to look worse than common when she went out begging. On the other hand, with a curious touch of womanly instinct, she always attempted to fix up a little. This time she had strapped back her lank hair with a piece of list, and pinned a man's cast-off paper collar around her scrawny neck. There were five hooks gone from the back of her tea-colored dress, and three others were straining to get loose, and give freer vent to the bulge of undergarment— once white, perhaps, but now of no particular hue—beneath. Her legs were bare half way down from her knees; and her big splay feet, in miserable shoes, that served no other purpose than to relieve her bony shanks, seemed to ally her with the waders and web-footed species.

Twinkle's little starry face shone out of her old wrap as peaceful as the blue March sky overhead. It was preposterous to try and make her look miserable. She left that sort of thing to luxurious infants, who are cppressed with their embroidered dresses and satin-lined cra-

dles.　She never appeared to think of what an
absurd little baby she was, pushing about, in a
child's weak arms, through the bustling streets.
She cogitated mainly on the jolly good noises
that every thing made.　The horse-cars, the
soap-fat man, the rag-gatherer's cart, fish-horns,
and fruit-venders, all seemed to be tooting, pip-
ing, and jingling for her especial benefit.

The poor little Crow had never been so happy
before in her life.　There was a great deal of
evil in the girl, I dare say ; but it had been
coaxed and petted, while every good trait that
attempted to peep out to the light got instantly
knocked on the head.　The heart that devoted-
ly loves a little child cannot be wholly bad, and
the Crow's love for Twinkle amounted almost
to adoration.　She had a sweet, maternal instinct in her bosom, that made her long for a
baby to pet and fondle.　Nobody would ever
trust their baby to her care, because she was
ill-favored and had a hard name.　That is the
world's way, you know ; when people are supposed to be bad they get fenced off from the
good, and left to grow worse and worse.　But
I do not believe that is the way our heavenly
Father deals with his misguided little ones.

The Crow, or Lindy, her true name, was the only lean bird belonging to her miserable mother's brood. There was no little brother or sister to mind. How often her hungry heart longed for one. Little Twinkle became a kind of lodestone to the poor creature. Nights, when she would lie down on her bunch of foul straw, supperless and cold—aching, perhaps, from the blows her tipsy mother had inflicted—an imaginary Twinkle would seem to come and creep into her miserable bosom, and her skinny arms would clasp the precious thought, forgetting that they closed on emptiness alone. God sends real or fancied comfort to the most wretched of his children ; and the Crow slept the sweet sleep of early life, believing that a pair of baby hands were cuddling in her neck, and a baby's sweet breath was warming her cheek.

Twinkle was never frightened, else I am sure she would have put up her lip when the Crow took her ; but to her dear, blessed eyes every thing looked beautiful and good. Accordingly they trotted out of Cork Alley together, quite unmindful of their professional duties, and bent on what Tom Malony called a " private bender."

There is a quiet corner even in this great rattling Gotham—Tobit Place, by name—a sort of acute angle, into which the whirling currents of life cannot conveniently run, although they do spill over there sometimes. Every thing in Tobit Place is just as it was twenty-five years ago. The Crow knew the spot, and liked it because it was warm and sheltered. Thither now she carried Twinkle. Then, sitting down on a door-step, she did a very curious thing for a Crow to do.

It was a pleasant March day. Can you believe it? There are some such days as pleasant as the pauses of a shrew's tongue. Every thing overhead was blue and sunny. Every thing in the vegetable kingdom was brown and bare, except the grass; but the very bareness and brownness of the tree-stems in Tobit Place had a softened look, as much as to say, " We are now ready for buds and birds."

The Crow was thinking of the little human bud in her lap, and thankful she had got where the wind could not nip her thin shoulders. The Crow had never had a real live baby in her arms before, and the woman germ in her led her to examine Twinkle's little body, and see how it differed from the very rudimentary forms she had given to her wretched rag infants, so she proceeded to unpin some of Twinkle's wraps and feel of her arms and legs. How that blessed child was turned and twisted and smothered face downward! But she did not as much as whimper. All the time her little rosy bud of a mouth was sucking away at her tiny flattened thumb with the utmost contentment.

When the Crow had come to the conclusion that the Lord could make a better baby than she was capable of manufacturing she began to talk baby talk, and to kiss Twinkle's lips and cheeks and the little plump hands, punctuated all over with good little dots. Her kisses were wild, hungry, starved kisses, that never could get enough. .

But at last this saintly infant rebelled, and the Crow did the most curious thing of all; she fell to crying, and rocked back and forth on the doorstep, with Twinkle pressed close up to her sharp ribs. Then and there she told the baby all about it, because she was "too blessed little" to know of herself, how she, the poor old Crow, got beaten and kicked around; how every body hated her, and she hated every body except Twinkle, and meant to drown herself to spite folks and make 'em bury her, only Twinkle wouldn't let her. She was too blessed little to know how ugly and hateful the old Crow was. "O! O! O!"

Twinkle did not relish these melo-dramatic weavings to and fro, and the hot tears that came plashing down on her cheek; so she set up a series of squeals, and began to kick with her feet through the old shawl.

"Hush, now, my oney-oney huney-puney." The Crow sat Twinkle upon her knee as straight as a cob. "Stop crying, and I'll unscrew my head and take out my eyes for yez to play with. 'Deed I will! We'll go to a swanny good place, like the outside of the cuccuses, and there we'll see the ladies a-jumpin' through hoops and the gentlemens a-hangin' by one foot."

"Ugh! ugh! ugh!" said Twinkle, looking excited, as if her infant mind was highly tickled with the picture. And I don't know but the pair might have moved away from Tobit Place in search of this rapturous spot if something had not happened.

The Crow was too busy to notice any body,

but every body was not too busy to notice her. There was a doctor's wagon before the opposite house. It was an old-fashioned concern, popularly known as a chaise. The house, too, was old-fashioned, with high iron posts bulging into something like a flower-basket on top, white marble steps, scrupulously clean, and ancient red brick walls.

The old lady who sat in the third-story front window, her neat muslin cap-border framing a fresh face, looked too busy and comfortable to be new-fashioned ; and the man who had drawn up the shade of the front parlor window as high as it would run, with his legs astride, and hands deep buried in his trowsers pockets, could hardly be called new-fashioned either. His hair had the peculiarity of always looking rumpled, and the corners of his mouth had a queer downward pull, that might indicate ill-humor or the love of dry fun ; but the upper part of his face—the brow and eyes—looked shrewd and observing.

" Massy sakes alive ! " exclaimd the old lady up in the third-story window as she happened to glance through her gold-bowed specs out into the street. " What witch-work is that girl about ! She looks crazy and acts more so ; but that baby in her lap is as pretty as the fust crocus."

Now the man in the front parlor window happened to be the Doctor to whom the wagon belonged ; and, oddly enough, he was looking for a baby. You wonder, perhaps, that he had to look far in a great city like this, that is just one vast nursery ; but the Doctor thought that he was a judge of babies, and it was not every specimen that would have suited him.

" What on earth is that girl up to ? " said the Doctor to himself as he watched the unconscious Crow. " She looks like an animated stable-broom, brush-end up. Whew ! that's a neat baby, though. Bet a copper it's been kidnapped."

He took his hat and strode across the street. Between the curtains at the back of the buggy peeped the eye of a young ebony, the Doctor's hold-boy.

" As I live, there goes John to speak to that girl ! " exclaimed the old lady in something of a flutter. " If I had on my hair front and my thicker boots, I'd go too and hear the confab."

However, she opened the window, and inclined her good ear to catch what she could from a distance. Gum, the hold-boy, was also taking notes.

As soon as the Doctor approached, Crow remembered her professional air, and held out her hand in a low-spirited manner.

" Please, sir, wont you help me and my little sister. We're poor orphins. Mother's sick at home ; father broke his leg last week, and had to go to the hospitable."

" O, you're orphans, are you ? Mother's sick and father's in the hospital, hey ? "

" Yes, sir ; that's the livin' truth."

The Doctor's face twitched, making it plain that the downward pull of his mouth was humorous, instead of ill-natured.

Twinkle was blowing great big blubbers with her bud of a mouth at the horsey-orsy and buggy-uggy over the way. Now she looked up into the Doctor's face and laughed—a bewitching baby accomplishment, that showed her pink gums, studded with three or four pearly teeth. This large, loose-jointed man had a strange fascination for babies, so he put one foot on the step, and his blunt-ended finger found its way to Twinkle's cheek, bringing happy gurgles and dimples in plenty, like a swarm of golden but-

terflies hovering about a rose. All this time
the Crow's professional snuffle went on, and her
grimy hand was held out for alms.

Suddenly the Doctor looked at her with his
shrewd, bright eye. "Where did you get this
baby?"

"She's my sister." The girl clasped Twinkle
fiercely.

"You lie." That was cool; but the Doctor
was a cool person. "Do you see that little
building down there," he continued. "Now
tell me all about it, or I'll whistle for somebody, and we'll have an examination."

The Crow knew this little building well. A
police officer was pacing back and forth before
the door. She shook with fear until her bones
almost rattled audibly; but she told the truth
about herself and about Twinkle, and the Doctor believed her. He took his finger away from
the baby, who was tugging at it with both her
puffy little hands, and called out, "Hullo! Gum,
wake up!"

Gum was any thing but asleep. He removed
his eye from the crack with a respectful "Yes,
sah;" and the next thing the astonished old
lady saw, from her perch in the third-story

window, was the Doctor putting that fright of a girl and the little fair-faced baby into his buggy. She threw up the sash higher, and screamed after him, "John! John! John!" with her cap-strings flying and her gold-bowed specs in great danger of tumbling off into the area. But he did not hear her, else I am sure he would have stopped and eased his mother's mind, who firmly believed he had gone crazy, for the Doctor was a good and dutiful son.

The wheels spun round on the noisy pavement, and away went that queer buggy load as fast as ever it could toward Mrs. Neuralgia's. Twinkle cried, "Goo! goo! goo!" and flapped her arms at the horse, believing she was in clover this time if never before.

Let us speed on ahead of them, and peer into Mrs. Neuralgia's sick chamber. Her house stands in a solemn corner, that always looks as if it were trying to repent of something; partly, I suppose, because Mrs. Neuralgia, being a rich lady, bribes the milkman to dispense with his unearthly hoot at her door, and pays the organ-grinders so much a month for skipping her neighborhood. She firmly believes a good healthy noise would kill her. In that house a

creaking door is a high crime and misdemeanor,
and any thing like a song, a whistle, or a baby's
crow, would be worthy of capital punishment.

We creep up the carved staircase, along the
padded hall, and enter her room through the
keyhole, in true spirit fashion. The apartment
is artificially close and shady. Every thing
about it seems sick, even to the handsome pictures and the rich carpet. There on the great
bed lies a pale, languid woman. Another silent,
watchful person moves like a ghost about the
chamber.

"Lewis," says a feeble voice, "have you got
on your lasting slippers?"

"No, ma'am. I made a mistake, and put on
my carpet-shoes."

"You know, Lewis"—there was a slight
touch of impatience in the sweet voice—"nothing but lasting suits my sensitive condition.
I thought I perceived a slight squeak about the
heels. It was torture to me."

"I'll change 'em directly, ma'am."

"That's right. Now take away these violets.
Their odor is too oppressive. I think, Lewis,
there must be the least little draught from that
window. Are you sure you caulked it perfectly

tight? Do light a taper and pass it before the cracks. A draught, Lewis, in my condition, would be my death-warrant."

Just then the front door banged with a prodigious report, and a pair of heavy stamping boots were heard coming up the stairs. Lewis uttered a suppressed scream and ran to the door. As for Mrs. Neuralgia, she gave a feeble shriek and went off into hysterics.

"O, Doctor, you've killed my mistress!" cried the maid, wringing her hands.

"Nonsense! Stand back! She needs air. She shall have air. That is all that ails her." He strode to the window, and with his great hand tore away all the swathings and caulkings, threw open the sash, and let a smart March breeze blow through the stale room.

The invalid hid her head under the blankets, and in a smothered voice cried out, "Doctor, you are a heartless assassin!"

"Monster!" exclaimed Lewis, striking a tragic attitude before him, and flourishing her arms almost too near his nose for her own personal safety.

"Wretch!" gasped Mrs. Neuralgia, more and more smothered under the clothes.

The Doctor sat down and laughed until the tears ran down his brown cheeks. Now there is nothing so exasperating as the laugh of a person that has wronged us, if we happen at the same time to be upbraiding him. Mrs. Neuralgia was dying to know why the Doctor laughed, so she made an excuse to breathe and looked out, her pretty, soft hair a good deal tumbled, and her face wearing an angry flush.

Instantly he checked himself, and arose as grave as a deacon. " My dear madam, compose yourself."

" Ugh! Sir, you may leave my house instantly, and never come back again."

" Now, my dear madam," (the Doctor could be very coaxing when he tried,) " do not jeopardize your health and happiness by a fit of pique. I have brought you a new remedy to-day, one I have long sought in vain to find. It has never been known to fail of curing such a case as yours."

Mrs. Neuralgia looked very cold, but she did not repeat her command ; so the Doctor coaxed more and more, and expatiated on the virtues of his wonderful new remedy. At last female curiosity prevailed, as he expected it would.

"And what may this extraordinary medicine be, sir?" asked the invalid, very stiffly.

"A baby, madam."

"O! O!" Mrs. Neuralgia screamed faintly; but she blushed more, and tried to look as if she meant to eat that horrible Doctor up, but failed badly.

"Lewis," said the Doctor to the maid, who was particularly savage, "go down to my buggy and bring up a baby you will find there."

Lewis knew when she must obey, as we all do when we find a master, so she went down. And Mrs. Neuralgia, I am sure, never before passed such a flustered minute and a half as the minute and a half that Lewis was absent.

When she came back, with the long end of Twinkle's old shawl hanging over her arm, and the Crow (such a picture—she had burst the last three hooks of her dress) following on behind, Mrs. Neuralgia exclaimed, with a gesture of disgust:

"Take away the ugly, dirty thing!"*

"Hold!" cried the persevering Doctor;

* See Frontispiece.

" flowers grow in the dirt. This is one of God's
human flowers, raised in a gutter, but just as
sweet and innocent as if it had budded in your
conservatory."   He slipped Twinkle, with these
words, out of a sheath of old rags, (her dress underneath was clean, though homely,) and laid
the little creature in Mrs. Neuralgia's bosom.
That bosom was loving and womanly in spite
of the imaginary aches and pains it had so long
petted.

In one minute's time Twinkle's cunning
little hand was patting and smoothing her
pretty white nest—we all know the power of a
baby's touch ; in two the hand had crept up and
made acquaintance with the sick lady's cheek ;
in three she was crowing, with all her dimples
on exhibition ; and before the expiration of five
minutes, as I live, Mrs. Neuralgia was sitting up
in bed, just as if she owned such a thing as a
backbone, holding Twinkle in her arms !

The upshot of it was, Twinkle cured Mrs.
Neuralgia, just as our wise Doctor said she
would. She had got an interest, now, outside
of herself—something to love and care for.
Accordingly, in a month's time she was a well
woman, going about her great, silent house, to

bang the doors and set every thing into brisk, merry motion.

Twinkle has got a nursery now, and plenty of fine toys, lace caps, and worked dresses, but she is the same even-tempered, winsome darling as before.

The Crow, whom people have learned to call by her right name, Lindy, has been washed, brushed, combed, dressed up in good clothes, and fed. O, it took a prodigious amount to "plumpen" her! as Tom Malony called the process; but the thing has been done, and she is now Twinkle's devoted nursery-maid. The sight of her earnest, happy little face is enough to make a chronic growler tear his hair.

Mrs. Neuralgia has extended her acquaintance down in Cork Alley, and about Thanksgiving time gets as far as Dublin-street and Backslum Corner, dropping her nice cards along, in the form of fat turkeys and chickens. It would seem as though she had adopted the whole Malony family. They have moved into nice sunny rooms, where it is easy to keep clean and be respectable. Mary has got a sewing-machine now, and she laughs a great deal more and scolds a great deal less than she used to. There is plenty of good food on the table, and warm clothing on the children's backs. As for Dennis Malony, he is dead and gone. Mary sighs as she looks at the black ribbon on her bonnet; but her heart is easy, for Dennis was only a stumbling-stone in this world, and we can safely leave him in our heavenly Father's keeping.

Tom and Sandy go to school now as regularly as clock-work. Every morning, when they pass Mrs. Neuralgia's with bright, rosy faces, they stop to kiss their hands to Twinkle, who is laughing in the window. Tom is at the head of his class, and, I think, rather expects some day to be President of the United States. If such a thing ever should happen, it is pretty clear in my mind that his old hen Speckle would receive the appointment of Secretary of State, and would grace the station, too, better than some of her predecessors. She has puuctually performed her duty ever since that memorable beginning made on the old refuse-barrel of the Crow's mother. Had that important event never occurred, it is plain to see the Crow would still be the same starved, unkempt creature she once was; the Doctor might at this

moment be looking for an infant ; Mrs. Neuralgia, in all probability, would lie nursing her selfish ailments in that close, shady room ; and our
dear sunshiny little Twinkle continue to play
the part of a professional baby.

MERCY DAVITS AT THE ANCHOR.

———— • ————

"THEE had better cut down the sign to-day, Jacob."

"So you aren't a-going to keep up the old tavern in no shape, Miss?"

"No! and thee can do as I bid thee," was the soft-voiced answer without amplification.

"Wal, now, how quare that seems for a Davits," responded the old man, in a drawling tone. "I've lived here at the Anchor, kept by a Davits, from the time I was a boy jest big enough to hold a gen'leman's horse, and now I'm gwine on seventy, and stiff in the jints. 'Taint likely the country folks are going to see the old tavern shet without opposition. I'm sorry to be obleeged to say it, Miss, but you'll make yourself onpoperler—and you be dead set, too, agin leasin' or sellin'. Dunk Ferguson was mightily put out because you wouldn't take up with his bid, and Dunk is an ugly customer when he gets riled. In course, if you say so, I must cut down the old sign, but it seems like hangin' my best friend. I shall be kind o' lost nights not to hear it creakin' and groanin' in the wind."

" Thee wont hear it any more," responded the new mistress, cutting short Jacob's long-windedness with admirable brevity and her own habit of coming to the point ; and then the little Quakeress, with quiet energy printed all over her small person, stepped again from the tavern porch within doors.

It was fifty years or more ago, before the days of railroads ; in fact, shortly after the last war with England, known as the war of 1812. The homely, low-browed tavern, with wide-spreading button-balls about the porch, had an inviting look to tired travelers, who journeyed mainly on horse-back, or in their own conveyances. Its small paned windows sparkled with cleanliness ; and the numerous chimneys, some, wen-like, plastered on the outside, and others rising from unexpect-ed places, were always smoking with a kind of savory invitation to a good meal. The Anchor was no low and slip-shod country inn. It had won a wide reputation for comfort and good cheer, and its prosperity and success were handed down as a heritage from father to son.

Many who had heard the fame of this old-fashioned public diverged some miles from the turnpike, and main traveled line, to share the comfort of its excellent beds and low-ceiled rooms, with their sanded floors, and heavy carved furniture shining from much hand polish.

A great change had come over the Anchor, and greater changes still were likely to follow. It had been regularly closed for three months, owing to the death of the old publican, Silas Davits, and for the first time in all its history had fallen to a woman; and the community, who had a stake in the old Anchor, were anxiously waiting to see what would follow.

Mercy Davits stepped out of the clear September sunshine into the best room of the public, the place which had always been reserved for fine company—the " quality "—ladies and militia captains, and circuit judges, and traveling parsons. It was wainscoted and ceiled with old oak darkened and mellowed by time; with deep window seats, great presses, and cupboards

for the best glass and china ; straight, high-back-
ed chairs of stiff and formal patterns, and curious
spider-legged tables. One side was taken up
with a vast chimney-piece and fire-place capable
of receiving the largest size back-log and fore-
stick, and making a glowing red cheer in a
winter day.

Back of this extended the inn kitchen, where
Lois Gibbs, the one hand-maiden that Mercy
had retained in her service, held sway ; and farther on was the stable-yard, with its huge barns
and sheds, and the horse-trough in the center
flowing over from a perpetual spring.

Above, in the second story, a ball-room extended the length of the house. It was the
best in the county, with a spring floor on which
old Silas Davits had specially prided himself.
There were also ranges of bed-rooms, furnished
with mighty high-posters, valanced and cur-
tained with dimity, and spread with gay patch-
work, that displayed the endless patience of
Mercy's grandmothers and great aunts, and
women of a later date belonging to the tribe of
Davits.

But, curiously enough, the apartment most
fascinating to the new mistress was the old bar-

room. It was strange that she should have fallen heir to such a place. A room solely devoted, through long years, to men—dedicated to their grosser appetites—had now become the property of one small woman.

A smell of stale spirits lingered about the place which slightly nauseated the new mistress of the Anchor, for she had a natural aversion to all intoxicating drinks. Still, she peered into corners and cubbies, as if trying to discern the charm which had drawn the old *habitués* to this spot, which had misled and ruined so many for whom her heart ached. The place should be whitewashed and cleansed, the bar itself and the shelves and bottle-racks taken down, and split up into kindling wood.

Further than this Mercy did not go. She was waiting for that deep inward manifestation of the Spirit, on which she had been taught to depend for guidance.

Wherever Mercy went about the house she could hear the blows of Jacob's ax as it ate its way into the heart of the old sign-post.

She had stepped out on the porch again to bid him split up the sign and kindle a fire with it on the best room hearth, as the day had grown suddenly cold, but stopped as she saw a traveler ride up on horseback and begin to parley with the old man. In another moment he was reining in his high-spirited, mettlesome horse by the inn porch.

He was a good-looking man, in the prime of life, with bright brown hair curling up under the brim of his hat, a straight nose, a forehead like ivory, a soft silk-brown beard, worn at a period when beards were not so common as they now are, and an eye that glowed at times with peculiar splendor. There was a certain vascillating, shifting expression about the lines of his face hard to define, and a shadow of weariness and languor would now and then cross it —like a little film of cloud dropped over a bright sky. He was dressed in the fashion of the day, top-boots and cape coat, and was powerfully and gracefully built.

"The new mistress, I presume," he said, slightly lifting his hat. "I am sorry to see yonder old sign come down," he added, in the tone of an impatient man who is easily moved to a certain depth. "It seems needless to incommode the public by shutting a place that has become a sort of land-mark to the whole country side. And now I suppose neither love nor money will purchase accommodation here for man and beast."

"Not if thee expects to be entertained as at an inn," said Mercy, firmly but mildly. " This place will no longer be kept open to the public, but I scarce shall deny any weary person the privilege of rest."

" Cold comfort that," returned the stranger, "for one who has been in the habit of taking his ease at his inn, as I have here at the old Anchor for the last dozen years, and my nag is so well used to stopping at this door whip and spur would not suffice to get him past. To speak the truth, I am myself as dry as a contribution box. I've lost my reckoning, the world seems turned topsy-turvy. I knew the old Anchor had changed hands, and there was a rumor of its falling to a woman, a granddaughter of old Silas Davits. The old man's sons all drank themselves to death, and more's the pity. They were the freest, best-hearted fellows to be met, but all a little weak in the head. Not one of them could keep his legs after the third bottle. I've made many a night of it with poor Will and Jerry and Stephen ; but they are all gone, and the old man went off in the tremens at last, tough as he was."

These last sentences he had uttered more to himself than to his listener, and looking up now with a softened expression, he added, " Pardon me ; this may be painful to you."

" I felt great concern for the state of my kindred," said Mercy, " though I saw them not in my youth, and gained all I knew from hearsay. My honored father was Hosea Davits, son of Silas, who separated himself from his people, and went out from among them."

" I well remember," said the stranger ; " he was the only pious Davits ever heard of. This tavern has been kept by a Davits for many genrations, and they have all been more famous for deep drinking than for much praying."

" Out of thy own mouth I find a reason for shutting this place," returned Mercy. " I am sorry to balk honest travelers, and where there is pressing need I will not deny them food and shelter ; but it is borne in upon my mind that I must not permit the sale of liquor here, where it has wrought much misery to many of my own name."

" A woman's crotchet," responded the other.

"Thee forgets," returned Mercy gravely, "not my will, but God's will."

"Well," said the stranger, "I think the whole country-side will rise and mutiny against your resolve to shut the Anchor, for where will the Circuit Courts be held, where will the coroner and his twelve men sit, where will the young folks come for junkets, and the old folks to hear the news and spin yarns?"

"I cannot tell thee, friend. I only know I must bear my testimony against the traffic of spirits, that much sin and crime may be done away."

"Don't speak so spitefully against good, honest drink," cried the other. "Many a glorious bout I have had in yonder room. You never have heard of me, I dare say; but I am Miles Corry, of the Pines; and it would indeed be a great accommodation to me and my beast if you would allow us to remain for the night."

"Thee is welcome to stay," returned Mercy, "if thee can content thyself with plain fare. If thee wishes thee can sit in the bar-room where those aforesaid glorious bouts were held."

"Come, come," said the other gayly as he swung himself off his horse, "you would bring me to repentance by leaving me alone to think over my sins. You would like to make a convert of such a reckless fellow as I am I'll be bound. Perhaps you yet hope to see me in a broad brim and a long-tailed drab."

"Thee may not be as reckless as thee would have it appear. There are those who put on an air of impiety to cover an aching heart. I do not think thee a blasphemer, or naturally a wine-bibber; but thee might use a round oath, or drink much too deep to seem as bad as thy company."

Miles colored and began to laugh, then checked himself and gave the little, quirt, drab figure before him a sharp look. "Shrewd, and wonderfully observing," he thought to himself.

Old Jacob had taken his horse away, and the guest, with his hands in his pockets, was strolling about the empty bar-room and whistling to keep his courage up. A restless, fidgety man ·like Miles Corry was not likely to stay long in such a place content with the companionship of his own thoughts. Before many minutes had passed he crossed the entry, and tapped lightly at the best room door.

"Come in," was the answer, and, opening the

door, he found Mercy on her knees blowing away at some kindling sticks in the deep fire-place.

"I thought, Miss Davits, you could not deny me a little of your company. I am but the worst possible comrade for myself at any time, and that other room is as dreary as a burying-ground on a dark night, full of ghosts and grave-stones."

"Thee may enter," was the reply, "but I would choose that thee call me Mercy, and I will call thee Miles, after the custom of my own people."

"I don't object in the least," said Miles, advancing into the room in his frank, easy, famil-iar way, and seating himself in a cushioned chair. "Mercy is a pretty name, but I fear it's small mercy you would show me if you had me in your power. You would cut off my bitters, and take away my toddy, and abolish all the beverages in between, that a dry and thirsty·soul craves. You would frown upon my pet follies and foibles, and clip, and shear, and prune me until I should not know my own face in the glass."

"Godliness is great gain," said Mercy, without any intimation of a smile in her eyes; in fact, she was deficient in the sense of humor, "but I would not have thee put on the outward semblance without the inward and renewing spirit, and that thee cannot get without loving something far better than thyself—without putting thyself under the guidance of duty."

"Duty go hang," laughed Miles. "I have always chosen to do what was agreeable to myself. My fond, doting mother gave me my way when I was a boy, and I have managed to get it ever since. There," he added, "is the old sign crackling in the flames. I can partly make out the faded anchor. They dance about as if they had a sinner in their clutches. I dare say that is the fate to which you would consign us poor worldlings."

"Thee should not misjudge me," said Mercy gravely. "I am in no way eager to thrust any human creature into the fire. And, perchance, it means only the undying heat and stress of remorse, that burns forever without consuming; neither am I so strait-laced by my creed as thee may suppose. Though I love the Friends' garb and plain language, still do I feel there may be those who attend steeple-houses, and dress in the guise of world's people, who strive after the higher life through a meek and quiet spirit. I will own unto thee that I cannot regard psalmody as some of my brethren do. There are times when I feel I must break forth into singing to give vent to the praise that rises in my soul like a fountain of living waters."

Miles, as he stirred the fire with a pair of tongs, looked furtively at Mercy, as if he had at last found what he had long been seeking, a new type of woman.

" I do not doubt your sincerity," he said, with involuntary respect, "but it's confoundedly inconvenient to have the old Anchor closed just now. I meant to make it my head-quarters in the coming canvass, and on election day to broach a cask of liquor on the green, and invite my friends and constituents to make themselves gloriously happy at my expense. You must know I am up for member of the next Congress. I bear a name much honored about here, for my father was a staunch man in Revolutionary days. For myself, I have not done any thing as yet but enjoy life. It has seemed so easy to do fine things I have hardly thought it worth while to try. But now my friends are bent on my making a figure in public life. The women compliment me specially with their patronage, but I never need look for flattery from you, Mistress Mercy."

"I should say," returned Mercy, studying him a moment, with her calm, steady eyes, "that thee is comely, with many gifts to win favors, but thee knows these things too well."

"And you are very plain of speech," returned Miles, slightly flushing.

"I could not tell thee a lie," returned Mercy, "and perhaps thee has not heard the truth spoken often enough for thy good. I would caution thee against supposing that obstinacy and a perverse will have caused me to close this place. Before I was brought to testify against the use of strong drink my heart was drawn to an inward stillness. Intoxication is the curse of this neighborhood. Every-where it is an open practice. The preacher, whose duty it is to warn and guide his flock, has liquors set out upon his sideboard, and offers them freely to all comers. So does Squire Wentworth, who lives in yonder stone mansion, and is counted a lamp and light in Israel. I would they might be pricked in the conscience, and made to see the error of their ways."

"I do not bother my head about the parson's shortcomings or the Squire's backslidings," said Miles carelessly; "but if you were to speak of the Squire's youngest daughter, Leah, that would be a different matter."

"Neighbor Leah Wentworth is known to me," returned Mercy.

"She is not a bad wench," Miles resumed. "She has a well-turned ancle, and a bright eye; and, even at the risk of strengthening your opinion of my conceit, I will tell you what every body knows already, that Leah is fond of me. I do not say but what I have given the girl some cause, but it's a perplexing business to know how to manage the women when you are so unfortunate as to be a general favorite. A good-natured man is apt to say more than he means, and to raise false hopes. There are times when little Leah wearies me, and I do not care a copper ha'penny for her, and other times she amuses me well enough. They say a de-termined woman can always marry the one she lays herself out to get, and perhaps Leah will be my fate after all. There is something positively frightful in the way an easy man like myself is subject to the other sex."

There was much in Mercy's face that remained unuttered, for just then a hand tapped the door. It was Lois Gibbs bringing in tea. Lois was a substantial, springless woman, who set her foot down very flat and toed in. She had the mouth and chin of a great talker, a persistent habit of putting in her oar, which Mercy was trying to curb, and an expression which denoted general and entire satisfaction with herself, and great immovableness of opinion.

"O, Mr. Corry," said she, setting down the tray, and dropping two or three "kerchies" in succession, "it's good for sore eyes to see you here once more. But times is changed, sir, sadly since the old boss died, and you used to be coming here to see Master Will and Master Steve, calling for your bottle free and hearty, like any gentleman should, and chucking the maids under the chin. And there was the old master always a bawling to the stable-boys, and coming to the kitchen to hurry up meals. There was plenty of noise and confusement then, sir, and a deal of fine company. You've got a beautiful stiddy head, sir. It's something to be proud on. I've seen you walk as straight as an arrer when most of the others was lying under the table. Them were glorious times, sir; but then things began to change. Master Will he went first, and his poor little foolish wife, she that was Abby Sprague, mourned herself to death up in the north-east chamber. Many a time, when I'd cook her a dainty to coax her poor appertite, she'd say, 'I couldn't eat a crumb, Lois, to save my life; there's a great load on my heart.'"

Lois came to a period for want of breath.

"Yes," said Miles, "the old days are past and gone, but I'll be bound your new mistress will treat you well."

"I've no fault to find, sir, but I've been used to excitement and having things lively, and it's hard to put up with a dull life, and nobody but old Jacob snoring in the chimney-corner of an evening."

Mercy gave her handmaiden a look which she must have understood, for the stream of loquacity suddenly dried up, and Miss Gibbs went out of the room.

The still fire was eating its way into the heart of the well-seasoned wood, and casting

long inquisitive beams into deep corners ; there
were wax candles burning on the mantle-piece,
and a little polished table stood between Miles
and Mercy that reflected the steamy, fragrant
silver tea-pot, and the best company china, set
out with a very nice and dainty array of Lois's
cookery. As she poured the tea Miles bethought
him to make a close and critical study of his
companion's face. There was a very pretty
light thrown upon it. It was comely and well
colored, with a pure skin, finely penciled eyebrows, a forehead squared a little by decision
and character, a gray eye, soft, yet penetrating,
a firm chin, a mouth red and well curved, and
by no means unkissable. The thick wavy tresses
of hair were drawn under a muslin cap of the
plainest pattern, and kerchief of the same was
folded across her bosom.

"You are younger than I thought," said
Miles, who had at last separated Mercy from
her demure costume and strange language.

"I am twenty six, if thee wishes to know,"
replied Mercy.

"And here I have been talking as if you
were the age of my grandmother."

"It is best thee should always think of me as

an elderly woman, for I have no taste for vain
and idle converse."

"I shall always be obliged to tell you the
truth," said Miles, "however much it may
damage me in your eyes." And then Miles bethought himself that it would be very interest-
ing to probe a little way beneath the Quaker
drab and set speech and find out what live emotions of womanhood inhabited his companion's
breast. He was prepared to begin the investiga-
tion when the light from a lantern flashed past
the pane.

"There now is my neighbor, Leah, come
with her father's old black serving man to pass
the evening."

"I though I caught a glimpse of Leah's face
at the window as I rode by the Squire's," said
Miles, with a shade of annoyance in his tone.

In another moment the visitor was in the
room. She was too demonstrative perhaps to
please Mercy, who freed herself as soon as she
could from the girl's embrace. Then there was
a little feigned surprise at finding Miles there,
which Mercy in her straightforwardness and
simplicity did not approve.

Leah had a pretty, round form, of whose

charms her scant, short-waisted brocade gown, in the fashion of the day, was perhaps somewhat too liberal. Her light hair had a trick of slipping out of the comb just at the right moment, and adding to the picturesqueness of her appearance by its billowy, wave-like masses. Her complexion was by no means perfect, nor were her teeth altogether regular. Her nose elevated itself slightly; but she had a pair of fine eyes, which she rolled up and used with admirable effect while making her sentimental little speeches.

"I came over to sit with you an hour, Mercy," said Leah, seating herself on a cricket by the fire, and pulling from her pocket a little scarlet purse which she was knitting. "I thought you might be lonely in this great, empty place, and would welcome even such poor company as mine, and here I find an old friend already before me."

"She was loth enough to take me in," said Miles, extending his feet lazily toward the heat, "but now I have gained a foothold I shall be apt to pester her pretty often."

"No wonder this old haunt has such charms for you still," responded Leah, with a slight lisp. "I always knew your attachments were ardent."

"Nonsense!" returned Miles, who loved to tease her. "I am as fickle as the wind, or a bee among clover. A pretty face never pleases me long. I am always ready to sip the dew from a fresh flower."

"Don't believe a word he says!" cried Leah, in a little characteristic outburst. "He has a good heart, take my word for it."

The deep red glow from the fire was shining on Mercy's quiet face and demure drab. The contrast could hardly have been greater than it was between her and Leah in her flowered brocade—her hair already down, and all the color about her coming to a focus in the bit of scarlet in her lap. Mercy was knitting a gray stocking, and as she turned the needle she said: "I dare believe Miles Corry is better and worse than he would make himself out."

"You need not expect her to flatter me," said Miles, who dearly loved to hear himself talked about, and to play off one woman against another. "She will tell me more plain home truths in an hour than I should hear in forty sermons ; and I do believe if I should get down on my knees to her, and beg for a glass of hot toddy, she would not feel even a twinge of pity for the infirmities of the flesh."

"Thee knows I have made a rule," was all Mercy said as she turned a needle.

"But you will break your rule this time?" coaxed Leah, getting hold of one of Mercy's hands. "What can there be so bad in a glass of bitters? My father takes his night and morning, and he is held in much estimation for piety."

"Thy father orders his house to suit himself," returned Mercy gently, "and so do I mine. There is One only to whom I must give an account of my stewardship. But were I ever so much disposed to give Miles the liquor, it is out of my power. There is not a drop of spirits in the house."

"Not a drop?" Miles repeated in astonishment. "To my certain knowledge there are, in the cellar, shelves filled with dusty, cobwebbed bottles worth their weight in gold, and great casks of wine that have never been broached."

"I have emptied every drop of their contents," replied Mercy, without a shade of emotion; "and thee must know that the poison spilled upon the ground will never burn the stomach or craze the brain of any human being."

"O, sacrilege!" groaned Miles. "To think of all that noble liquor wasted! That priceless stuff that has been ripening and mellowing, gathering tone and color for years, thrown away! I wonder old Silas Davits, who stored it and prized it as the apple of his eye, did not groan in his coffin! But, speaking seriously, I fear this rash act will give you trouble. Dunk Ferguson, I understand, is very angry because you refused to lease him the place. He is a kind of leader among the desperate, rough characters, of whom there are many in this neighborhood, and if he should bring them here some day in a half-intoxicated state, there is no telling what the devil might tempt him to do."

"But what harm could he devise?" inquired Mercy, looking up.

"He could burn the old tavern over your head, and he would not scruple if his blood was up."

"I shall go forward in the way the Lord has appointed," was Mercy's answer.

"And do you think a miracle will be performed on purpose to aid you?"

"I know not," the reply came, after a moment's pause. "I see the path of duty plain before me. What the consequences to myself may be I cannot stop to consider."

They all sat silent for a time, and then Leah rose to go home, and Miles offered to accompany her. Mercy stepped into the kitchen to light her lantern.

"She's a stiff old maid, isn't she?" whispered Leah.

"Not so much older than yourself; and were it not for her Quaker cut she would be a handsome little woman."

Leah turned her back and began to pout, but Miles managed to dispel the jealous fit by stealing a kiss. The way to Squire Wentworth's was not long. Miles was absent an hour or more, and before he returned Mercy had disappeared. The next morning Lois gave him an early breakfast, and he rode away without seeing the mistress of the Anchor.

A fortnight passed away peacefully enough. The first hard frost had come to sear the fields; the October tang was in the air, and the woods flushed with many colors. Old Jacob came haltingly into the presence of Mercy. The cold snap had given a tightening screw to all his joints.

"I thought I ought to let you know this is muster day," whined he. " The train-bands will be out with flying colors, and all the rag, tag, and bobtail at their heels. The old master always expected a big carouse on trainin' day. Dunk Ferguson may come here and threaten wiolence unless liquor is brought out. Now, hadn't I better get down the old shot-gun from the garret, overhaul it, and put in a primin'? It's the same trusty arm that one of the fighting Davits, long ago, tuk intu the Revolution. It kicks pretty bad, and misses fire nine times out of ten ; but it might scare some o' them scalliwags to see it pinted out of the window."

"God forbid," said Mercy, "that I should meet violence with violence. Does not the good Book bid thee bless them that curse thee, and do good to them that despitefully use thee, and if any man smite thee on the right cheek to turn to him the left also?"

"Dunno," said Jacob, scratching his head, "I'm no great Bible scollard. I could tell you more about the pints of a horse. But I favor old Leviathan law, an eye for an eye and a tooth for a tooth. If any man should whack me on the cheek, I'd be pretty apt to whack him on the jowl."

The morning hours slipped quietly by, and the short autumn day was drawing to a close, when Lois and Jacob rushed in with frightened faces to announce that the roysters were coming down the road as tipsy as loons.

"They've half fuddled themselves at Poole's on the Pike," explained old Jacob, in a nervous tremor, "and now they're calling for drink here, like so many dry devils."

"Go and tell them," Mercy's low voice was scarcely raised at all, though her face was a shade paler, "to get quietly away from here or they will suffer the penalty of the law." .

"There aint no law they're afeard of," whined the old man. "Dunk rides rough-shod over the Justice when he's in liquor, and he likes a drop too well himself to fine him over a few shillings. They hate a Quaker like pison. Nothing but the old shootin' iron would do a mite o' good."

"I bid thee go and command them in my

name to leave this place, and not to break the peace."

Jacob must needs obey, though he quaked in every limb; and the mistress of the Anchor, by a supreme effort of will, stayed where she was, within doors. It seemed as though her heart stopped beating as she strained her sense of hearing to catch the sounds from without.

Then came the tramping of feet, a burst of wild singing, and afterward jeers, and hoots, and drunken curses, as Jacob attempted to speak. The clamor grew into an uproar, above it were shrieks of the old serving-man. In an instant Mercy had darted through the hall, up the stairs, and out upon a balcony that projected from the second story window. Below her was a rabble of lewd fellows in every stage of intoxication. Some of the lads, mere boys, were decked in cock's feathers and paper epaulets. Dunk Ferguson carried a cudgel, and was flourishing it about old Jacob's ears, choking the old man, who hung down white and limp by his neck-handkerchief.

Dunk was powerfully built, with a fiery face, heavy jaw, straight black hair, and a very restless evil eye.

The moment Mercy stepped forward on the balcony, and lifted her hand to speak, a yell went up from the reeling crowd that effectually drowned her voice.

"We'll stop your mouth, you canting Quaker," cried Dunk with an oath and the action of a fiend, and instantly sticks, stones, brick-bats, old bottles, any thing and every thing the gang had armed themselves with or could pick up from the road, began to fly through the air. The glass of some of the windows was shivered to atoms.

In the midst of this demoniac din, all aimed and directed at herself, stood Mercy, with her hand uplifted as if turned to stone. The missiles flew mostly wide of the mark, owing to the extreme tipsiness of the assailants, else her danger would have been imminent.

Dunk Ferguson had just proposed to batter down the door and open the cellars in search of liquor, and to see whether the Quaker woman had lied, when Mercy, as in a nightmare, saw a figure spurring along the road, plunging his rowels deep in the sides of his foaming beast. Instantly, like a flash of light, Miles Corry was in the midst of the rabble. She saw the butt end of his heavy riding whip descend with light-ning speed about the head and face of Dunk Ferguson. Once, twice, three times it came down, and then there was a great, ugly gash, and the man's dark cheek was streaming with blood.

Mercy was sick with horror, but she saw and heard all. Dunk, down on his knees, was shak-ing his fist in the air.

"I'll take my revenge out of your flesh and blood, Miles Corry. I'll take it out of your heart."

"You whelp, you cur, you mean, dastardly sneak," cried Miles, pale to the very lips, "to dare come here and attack a defenseless woman. I'll see you grinning through the bars of a cage before many days are over."

Dunk, faint from loss of blood, fell over upon his side, and some of his companions, who could walk with a degree of steadiness, hurried him away down the road. The place was cleared of the rioters in less than five minutes. One straggler, a ragged, hatless fellow, had fallen down under a tree, and was left behind.

Mercy had gone down into the road, and Miles, who had followed the retreating rabble but a few paces, turned eagerly back to inquire if she had escaped without hurt.

"I have not a scratch upon me," she replied in a faltering voice, reaching him her hand, and pressing his gratefully. "In the good providence of God I owe my safety to thee. This day's work has wrought a bond between us I shall never forget. It has made me thy friend through evil report and through good report. Though I deplore the shedding of blood, I can but deem it noble in thee to so venture for my sake."

"Pooh," said Miles lightly, more affected by her look and tone than he was willing to show. "It was nothing. I thought no more of it than scattering a herd of swine."

"Now thee sees the evils of strong drink, as I do, thee has, perchance, come over to the help of the Lord against the mighty."

"No, nothing so fine and grand as that," returned Miles, smiling languidly. "I would strike a hard blow to defend a woman when I would not lift my finger from what you term principle, or even to serve myself. But you will let me rest an hour with you here at the Anchor, and give me a cup of tea and a bite of some-

5

thing to eat, for, to tell you the truth, I am dog tired and half famished."

Lois Gibbs, during the assault, had stationed herself in a window and uttered a succession of screeches, as if a pin were being driven into her side at regular intervals. She was now back among her pots and pans, and old Jacob had crept out of the stable, where he had hidden himself, with his hair full of straw.

"I thought I was dead as a nit," he sniffled in a piteous tone.

"Dead man!" said Miles, "you haven't a scratch about you."

"The breath was all choked out of me, and I sha'n't get my wind again for many a day."

"You retained the use of your legs wonderfully well, and your old back should smart for running away and leaving your mistress to face those fiends alone."

"It was my head," returned Jacob; "I was quite dazed, and when I come to I found myself in the barn under old Dobbin's heels."

"Well, bestir thee now," said Mercy; "I want thee to fetch me in that man by the road side yonder and put him to bed."

Jacob stared at her with open mouth.

"What, that coot, Tim Sackett, the greatest sneak-thief and vagabones in all the country? Put him into one of the beds at the Anchor? Why he deserted, and come near dangling from the end of a rope in the war. He's never sober three days together, and many a time I've seen the old master thrust him out in the cold when he had no money to pay his score, and his wife, too, for that matter. She used to come, crying and complaining that the children starved at home, because Tim spent all his wages and her own here at the Anchor."

"Then am I more bound to give him shelter," said Mercy, "if he was tempted here, and led into evil habits that stole away his manhood."

"I didn't think of it in that there light," returned Jacob, scratching his head. "I can remember when Tim Sackett was a likely young man, with as fair chances as any body, till he took to carousing round the tavern here. But he's a bad egg now, not decent to sight or smell, and if I was you I'd let him lie in the stable."

"Do as I bid thee, and bring him in," was Mercy's reply.

Miles Corry had still some distance to ride that night before he slept. As he was mount-

ing by the light of a candle which Mercy, standing on the porch, held and screened from the
wind with her hand, she said to him in an anxious tone.

"I tremble, Miles, at the risk thee runs from
that bad man."

Miles's face was in shadow. Stooping over
the saddle-bow, he took Mercy's hand and
pressed it tenderly.

"Never fear for me. I have given the scamp
a quietus for the present, and before he gets
lively again about Satan's business I mean to
bestir myself to have him imprisoned for a term
of years."

Mercy stopped a moment to listen to the
clatter of Miles Corry's horse's hoofs down the
dark road. As she was turning in again, where
the fire-light shone through the bedroom windows, she caught sight of a figure crouching in
the deep shade of the porch, and partly screened
by the trunk of a large tree.

"Who is lurking there?" she called, startled
by the remembrance of the possibility that
some of Dunk's men might come back to fire
the house, or work other mischief. She was
answered by the feeble wail of a sick child, and

a woman's form crept nearer the little dim circle
of light made by his candle—a crouching, dead-
white looking woman, with a tattered shawl
about her shoulders in which a baby was
wrapped, while a wild-eyed, bare-footed little
boy clung to her skirts.

"O, marm," moaned the woman, crouching
still lower, "I'm not hiding round here to do
you any mischief. I was forced to come out
with these little ones, leaving the two oldest at
home to look for my man, Tim Sackett. May
be you've seen him hereabouts. He's quite
lost when in drink, and might wander here un-
beknown, for his feet would take the way to
the tavern of themselves. This little one in my
arms is bad in the head, and the boy is croupy.
I couldn't leave them behind, and I couldn't
stay at home. If Tim is off on a spree I'm like
a crazy creeter in a cage. I've been druv out
to look for him in the snow and in the rain, in
the heat and in the cold. I've been afeard I
should come across his dead face starin' up at
me from the ditch, and I couldn't be held with
an iron chain. He never spoke a harsh word
when he weru't in liquor, marm. He feels so
sorry for what he's done, he takes to drink agin

to drown the thoughts of where he's brought
me and the children down to.   There's the oldest boy and girl home now without a morsel to
eat, or a bit of fire or candle-light, and they
too little to sense much.   They sob themselves
to sleep in the dark.   O you feel as if your
heart was cut in two with a sharp knife when
your man is lost, and you must go seek him,
leaving the children to cry at home."   ,

"Thee has, indeed, told a piteous story,"
said Mercy, wiping a little trickling tear from
her cheek ; "I am glad to tell thee thy husband
is here, I have had him cared for, and thee need
go no further to-night.   Take thy children to
the kitchen and dry thee by the fire, and get a
taste of hot supper and what thee needs for the
little ones."

"Are you an angel?" asked the woman,
looking up wonderingly into Mercy's face as
the light of the candle flickered over her white
cap and pure cheek.

"Nay," said Mercy, "a poor, weak, erring
mortal like thyself, and doubtless far less than
thee ; for, like the woman of Scripture, thee
has loved much."

Tim Sackett's wife, looking more cowed and

dead-white than before, was seated before the generous blaze of the kitchen hearth drying her garments, soaked with the night dew. Mercy had taken the rickety baby from its mother's arms, and the little spindling boy, with his bare, brown feet, and great hungry eyes, was watching and smelling the processes of frying and short-cake baking with infinite satisfaction.

Lois went about banging the kitchen utensils, and violently opening and shutting doors—her favorite mode of showing disapproval of the higher powers.

" I can't and wont stand it," she exploded, raiding out on the shed whither Jacob had retired to smoke his clay pipe in peace. " It was too much for flesh and blood to bear when Tim Sackett was put between clean sheets, them I bleached in June grass with my own hands, and now the rest of these lousy, vagrom Sacketts is brought in for me to cook for. I'll clear the coop agin' morning comes."

" No, you wont," returned Jacob calmly. " The new mistress is a quare un', that's certain, and you will have to bile over like the tea-kittle about once in so often ; but you aint going to quit this place on that account any more than the tea-kittle is going to quit the fire. The place is too easy, and the pay is too reg'lar and, as I've often justly remarked, there's too many requisites."

Before many days it was pretty well known, much to the astonishment of the neighbors, that Mercy Davits had taken in the whole Sackett family—had not only fed and clothed the wretched wife and half-starved children, but had actually undertaken to give Tim, who was very contrite and penitent, a chance to reform. The rear part of the old tavern stand was made into a habitation for the family. Mercy had inherited along with the house a farm of some extent ; she proposed to furnish Tim employment, in cutting wood and tending cattle, sufficient to keep those dependent on him and save him from temptation.

The scheme seemed so wild and impracticable that Miles Corry, who was spurring about the country these bright autumn days on electioneering business, and in efforts to bring Dunk Ferguson to justice, called to expostulate.

"I tell you," said he, striding about the best room and switching his top boots with his riding whip, " Tim Sackett's stomach is burnt to a cinder ; he will rob and cheat you, no doubt, and then return to wallow in the mire."

" I will have patience," returned Mercy. " Thee knows that faith can move mountains. But it moves them, I take it, an inch at a time. I will be content with small results. Would it not be enough to save one child from a life of misery, and here are four. little ones gathered under my wing."

" A woman like you," said Miles, glancing at her furtively, " must waste herself in some direction or other. If she does not throw herself away on a worthless man, she will do it on beggars and lazy good-for-naughts. It appears to me she is wiser to offer the sweet sacrifice of her devotion to some cleaner and more respectable member of my own sex than Tim Sackett."

A slight blush rose to Mercy's cheek as she said in a low voice,

" Thee should remember I strive to follow the leadings of the Spirit."

Though Miles exerted himself in the matter, Dunk Ferguson was not brought to trial before election day. Ruling by rum, he made himself felt and feared ; and at that time the machinery

of justice was slow in getting into operation.
Although Dunk was still at large he was under
a cloud, and dared not present himself at the
polls, held three miles away at Poole's, on the
Pike. The result was Miles Corry triumphed.
There was no actual breaking of heads on the
occasion, but much rough roystering and horse
play, and a deal of hard drinking, in which the
successful candidate freely participated.

It was late on the same afternoon. The sun
had set, and a still glow pulsed up the sky,
and gleamed like an inlet to Paradise between
the spectral tree stems of the little wood where
Mercy Davits was walking. She had gone on
a visit to a sick neighbor, and, belated, was
hurrying home the nearest way across the fields.
Her light step and scant skirt scarce rustled the
fallen leaves. She had almost reached the road,
which was itself solitary and deeply shaded,
when the sound of familiar voices struck her ear.
It was easy to peer through one of many open-
ings in the bare boughs at the path beneath.
Miles Corry had dismounted, and was leading his
horse with the bridle thrown over one arm,
while the other encircled Leah Wentworth's
waist. His rich dress was slightly disordered.

His handsome face was flushed with wine, the breath came hot through his lips, and his eyes glittered with excitement. Leah's scarlet hood had slipped back from her bright hair, and she was gazing up into his face.

"O stay with us to-night, Miles!" Mercy heard her say, "my heart misgives me at the thought of your long ride through the woods."

"What a timid little puss you are," returned Miles lightly. " There is nothing to fear from that whipped dog, Dunk Ferguson. He did not even dare to show his ugly face at the polls to-day. It was a glorious victory, and I must ride home to carry the good news to my old bed-ridden mother, who will be ready to die of joy now that her lazy son has turned out at last good for something. The men at Poole's were bent on my staying to make a night of it, but I slipped away quietly, and left them to drink my share for me."

" And is it true what you just now said, that you do indeed love me ? You have told me so many times before, but have forgotten the words when some fairer face came between us."

" Of course I love you," returned Miles ; "and

do you know you look bewitching in this
light, Leah—lovely enough to drive any man
out of his sober senses." He clasped her waist
more closely, and pressed hot, impassioned
kisses on her lips.

"And will you keep your promise, and make
me your wife," asked Leah in a low voice.

"Yes, yes ; if I ever marry at all, until I am
a gray-beard. How can I now, just entering on
my career in life, pluck out my brightest feathers,
and become a tame fowl to mate even with such
a little singing bird as you are?"

"There," cried Leah, catching at a straw,
"you have promised me, and we are betrothed."

"Well, have it so," said Miles, laughing, and
he kissed her again ; "but go home now to your
father. Don't trust any man too far, or believe
too implicitly in his promises," and he leaped
on his horse and was off down the dusky road
like a whirlwind.

The stars had not yet began to shine, and
only a few scattered gleams of daylight remained. Something touched the girl's arm
lightly, and she turned with a slight scream.

"Thee need not fear, it's me, Mercy Davits."

"And so you have been watching and spying

on us," cried Leah, with a sudden irrational burst of anger.

"Hush!" responded Mercy in a low voice, "I chanced upon thee and thy companion, and unwittingly played the eaves-dropper."

"Then you heard what he said," the girl eagerly exclaimed. "You heard his vows and promises. You must have seen him embrace and kiss me."

"But he was heated with drink," replied Mercy sadly, "and it is said that vows made in wine are writ in water."

"Perhaps you love him yourself," cried Leah, taking told of Mercy's arm, somewhat rudely. "I never more than half trusted your soft ways. But he is mine; promise me you will not be so wicked as to come between us."

Mercy stood quite still for a moment with her eyes bent upon the ground. Perhaps her face blanched a little, it was difficult to tell in the deepening dusk. "I promise thee," she whispered at last, "and may the Searcher of hearts keep mine steadfast."

In that long, dark prelude to a November morning, which dawned at last chill and gray, Mercy was awakened by a knocking upon the

outer door, violent at first, then interrupted, and
mingled with what seemed a broken moan. She
threw on a few garments with her heart in a
tremor of apprehension, and went down hastily
to undo the door. As it opened, a person sitting on the step fell back against her knees. It
was Leah Wentworth, her face wild, white, and
scared, and drawn with agony.

" Father in heaven, what ails thee ? "

" Miles," groaned the girl, " is murdered—he's
dying. The assassin met him there in the dark
wood, and as he was riding home, so happy and
gay, full of hope, with my kisses on his lips, thinking of me, perhaps ; and he was shot three times
and left for dead, lying on the damp leaves and
moss, with his life-blood oozing away. Dunk
Ferguson did it, they say, and he has escaped.
The riderless horse went home with blood on
his flank, and the search began. I could not
stay there in that house. I don't know where
I have been stumbling about in the dark. I
don't know why I came here, for I never loved
you, and sometimes I've almost hated you."

The words came between gasps and sobs
The girl's little flimsy affections were all torn
away. She was lying at Mercy's feet with her

long damp hair about her. The mistress of the
Anchor must have uttered a cry that woke old
Jacob and Lois. But she quickly gathered
Leah up in her arms, and half carried her into
the best room, and sitting down held her with
her head pressed close against her bosom. The
thick hard sobs, each one coming painfully, as
if it drew a certain portion of her life with it,
shook Leah's whole body. What was passing
in Mercy's breast is difficult to say.

"Hush, child!" she whispered hoarsely,
"God's will be done. Thee must not rebel."

"God has no right to take him away from
me," Leah cried passionately. "He is cruel,
cruel, and relentless, and not a God of love.
You, Mercy Davits, have never loved, or you
would not speak such words to me; they are
hard and cold as icicles."

The poor girl's words died away in disjointed
sentences and broken moans. Mercy felt of
her head. It was burning like fire, while her
hands were ice. The lethargy of brain fever
was approaching. Just as dawn broke over the
frosty fields, with the help of Lois she carried
Leah into her own room, undressed, and put
her to bed. Old Jacob had been dispatched to

gather tidings of Miles Corry's fate, and send over to the Anchor Leah's eldest sister, a spinster, who kept house for the old Squire. She came by sunrise, and then began a long vigil beside the sick girl's bed.

Leah was in the grasp of a dull stupor, with a dark and sinister flush on her face. She moaned, and tossed her arms out of the clothes, and the breath came painfully through her baked lips. Mercy had not taken off her gown, or laid down, and it was the afternoon of the second day. There were ashen rings about her weary eyes, and her face was so colorless it seemed as though a tinge of red could never visit it again.

On the afternoon of the second day Leah opened her eyes with a sane look in them, and Mercy bent over and whispered, " Miles will live. The doctors are sure of it. Comfort thyself with the thought."

And Miles did live, though his recovery was so slow as to be almost hopeless. Dunk Ferguson had been caught, tried, and sentenced to imprisonment for life before Miles could leave his bed. The winter had come on, stern and pitiless, with whirling storms and vast snow-drifts.

Scarcity of money and a short harvest the previous summer were causing wide-spread distress. Rye and Indian bread was eaten, even on the Squire's table. The white loaf had quite gone out of fashion. Mercy had kept Tim Sackett, and taken in three other families, all of them with intemperate husbands and fathers, destitute, and out of work. The finger of the Lord seemed plain to her now, pointing out the road she ought to travel.

Mercy had used every available room which she could spare in the old tavern stand for her strange community. The great ball-room was partitioned off into living apartments. There were more than a dozen children in all. The fuel her own woods supplied. By dint of utmost economy, and good management, she was able to furnish her little colony with food. The other women were even more discouraging than Tim Sackett's flabby, broken-spirited wife. They were slatternly and unneat, with the bad habits which poverty, misery, and the custom of living from hand to mouth had ground into them. Mercy undertook to teach them how to keep their rooms, to cook, to sew, to care for and instruct their children. Now and again, one or other of the men went on a "spree," but not so often, perhaps, as might have been expected. There were trials and drawbacks all along the path ; but still Mercy, with her calm, clear eyes, could look up, and bless God for his mercies. The power of rum was gradually dying out of that neighborhood.

One day in early spring, when the fields were bare, the sky blue, and roads heavy with mire, Miles Corry reined his horse in by the tavern porch, and slowly dismounted. He was pale, shrunken within his clothes, bent in the shoulders, and very tremulous and weak. He stopped awhile outside in a long coughing fit. It was after Mercy had helped him in, and removing his wraps, had seated him in a great chair by the fire, that he attempted to speak.

"Why do you suppose I came here to-day, Mercy?" he asked, looking at his bloodless hand.

"To give me the joyful assurance that thee still lives in the flesh," she answered, with a tender suffusion of the eyes.

"No, no, no," said Miles impatiently. "I am not handsome enough to wish to show myself. I came expressly to ask you to be my wife. It

is what I have been thinking of all these terrible months, when the pain would let me think
at all."

Mercy was perhaps violently startled, but she
did not show it, save by a slight tremor in the
hands and a delicate blush which overspread
her face.

" I cannot marry thee, Miles Corry," she began
in her usual plain, pointed manner of speech.
"I am no yoke-mate for thee; besides, the
Friends meeting forbids its members joining
themselves unto world's people. This is only
a sick fancy which will pass away when thy
vigor returns."

"I tell you it is not," replied Miles, almost
angrily, the hectic of weakness coming into his
face. "I don't pretend to be a much better
fellow than I was before this happened. My
faults have not been all burned out of me. I
am not religious, and I am selfish, perhaps, in
asking you to take up with a poor broken wreck.
But my youth is over, Mercy. It died that day
my enemy met me in the wood, when I was so
lusty, so full of life, so confident of myself. I
am only feeling out blindly now for a support
and shelter, for something to believe in, to

cling to, to rest upon, and I reach my arms toward you."

" There is one you have kissed and promised. I saw you that day when you did not see me," said Mercy in a low voice.

"O, yes, Leah Wentworth," he answered carelessly. " All that belongs to the dead past. It is over and done with. I have trifled with many women in my time; I never thought there was much harm in it. You were the first one I was forced to respect thoroughly, and now I have learned to reverence you. You will save me from myself. You are my only hope, my only salvation," and he bent toward her with his wan, pleading face, and outstretched hands.

" Nay," said Mercy, growing pale, " thee cannot put behind thee the consequences of the past, thee cannot get away from them. The sin of breaking a young heart and crushing a life must not rest on thy conscience."

"I know Leah loves me," returned Miles impatiently, "but she always makes her love plain. She wore her heart on her sleeve, and that day coaxed a promise from me when I hardly knew what I was saying."

" But thee had promised before, thee had

promised often,"—said Mercy relentlessly, "and now the girl will die unless she gets comfort and hope from thee. She has long been sick, and is greatly changed, chastened, and softened ; a wiser mind has come. She is only the same same in loving thee still too fondly."

"Poor Leah! is it indeed so?" returned Miles. "The pleasures I once thought so fine, come now and scowl at me with the faces of ugly old sins. I will do what I can for Leah, but you must take back those hard words. You said you would never marry me."

A gleam of the old fire returned, the determination to have his way and ride over all opposition. He sprang up, seized Mercy's hands, held them hard, and probed her eyes with his own.

"Tell me if indeed you do not love me, O tell me the truth?"

Mercy, by a great effort, seemed to force all the blood in her body back upon her heart.

"No, not as Leah loves thee. I could not give my soul to pleasure thee."

Miles dropped her hands and walked away coldly toward the window, and moodily rubbed his chin as he looked out at the blue sky cumbered with masses of white clouds. Mercy came softly behind him with his hat and furred great coat.

"It is time for thee to go to Leah," she began. "The poor child must have seen thee ride past, and is doubtless waiting and watching at the window, heart sick with hope deferred."

"You talk as if I were mortgaged, and about to be sold," returned Miles in a savage tone.

"Nay," she faltered, "act well thy part, do thy duty, learn obedience"—and then her voice died.

"You are cruel, cruel; but I will obey you," he cried; and he turned and clasped her in his arms and kissed her. It was the first and last kiss.

Long after he was gone Mercy moaned in her pain. She alone knew how great had been the temptation. She alone knew that afterward angels came and ministered unto her.

AUNT THORBURN'S BLANKET SHAWL.

———•———

"DON'T go yet, Henry; I must have a check this morning."

Mr. Preston had his hand on the door-knob, prepared to quit his handsome up-town residence for his down-town place of business.

"A check, Clara? Didn't I give you one on Brewster's for three hundred dollars less than a fortnight ago?"

"Yes, I know you did; but I was obliged to use most of it to pay back debts. Madame Pulsifer is very pressing, and says she must have the money for my moire and poplin suit this week."

"Confound the old turk! You have paid her thousands of dollars. She isn't decent in her charges; you know she isn't. You ought not to put up with such swindling. It's enough to ruin a millionaire."

"I know, Henry, her bills are enormous; but nobody gives me such splendid fits as she does."

"I'd like to give her fits, the old leach!" muttered Mr. Preston petulantly as he opened the door and stepped into the vestibule. "I can't attend to it this morning, Clara; you must wait until I come up to-night." He slammed the door in a way to make the plate glass shiver unpleasantly and was gone.

"O dear!" sighed Mrs. Preston, knitting her pretty brows. "I do wish Henry would be reasonable. , I am sure no one in my position can do with less than I have, although he sometimes accuses me of extravagance. He would be the very first one to complain if I did not dress —and quite as well, too, as anybody in our set."

The elegant little lady turned her head to note the hang of her white morning dress, where the rich festoons of her train lay coiled upon the velvet carpet. Then she glided into the drawing-room—frescoed and garlanded, upholstered and adorned with pictures—and glanced up at the mirror, that looked like a crystal cave in a fringe-work of ferns and dainty woodland things, carved from black walnut.

The pretty face which the polished surface reflected still had a cloud upon it that hinted at the absence of perfect bliss even in such a little paradise as that drawing-room was. However, Mrs. Preston set straight her dainty little point-lace cap, and smoothed out her rose-colored ribbons, and twisted the bracelet on her delicate wrist, until the consciousness that she was very pretty and stylish, and that her morning costume became her to a charm; dissolved the cloud to a very thin mist indeed.

"Robert," said Mrs. Preston, turning toward the man waiter, who stood in the dining-room, near the blaze of a soft-coal fire, that flickered upon the glass and silver of the yet uncleared breakfast table in dozens of crimson gleams.

Robert, a very clerical-looking character, in a white choker, turned like a grenadier and bowed.

"Robert, if Madame Pulsifer's young·man calls this morning say I am out."

Robert bowed again.

"And, Robert, order the carriage for three this afternoon."

Again that functionary inclined his person.

"And tell Fanny not to bring the children down until lunch-time."

A third time the process was repeated silently.

Mrs. Preston sank back in a stuffed easy-chair—a veritable Sleepy Hollow of padding and brocatelle—and put out her daintily-slippered feet toward the fender. She sighed once or twice—without noticing Robert, who was stealthily removing the cloth—in a manner that showed something more than the mere butterfly burden of a fashionable woman's existence was weighing upon her thoughts; nevertheless, she shifted the cluster diamond ring on her slender forefinger, and watched to see it throw off sparkles of iridescent color in the blaze of the firelight.

Perhaps, if the little woman's thoughts had found utterance, they would have run somewhat in this wise: "O dear, how I wish I had an independent fortune of my own! It is horrid to be always short for money! How I hate to ask Henry for what is actually necessary to meet expenses. And, then, it is so humiliating to have him look cross, and talk as he did this morning. I degrade myself in the eyes of trades-

people when I put them off with trumped-up
excuses, and feel as though my own servants
look down upon me. But what can I do?
Henry would scold worse than ever if I did not
dress to his taste; but I sometimes think I
would gladly sell my diamonds, and go about
clad in fustian, for the sake of being independent
in money matters."

She petted and caressed the beautiful cluster
on her finger with a heroic, high-toned feeling,
as if she were entitled to an immense amount
of credit for merely thinking of such a sacrifice.

Just then the door-bell ting-a-linged, as door-
bells are apt to ting-a-ling in aristocratic man-
sions.

"Stop, Robert," she said as that functionary
was about to obey the summons. "Dear, dear!"
she went on to herself; "there is Mrs. Brace,
with those tickets for the charity concert, and
I have scarcely a dollar in my purse. Robert,
if Mrs. Brace has called say that I am out."

Robert bowed, and a blush of shame tinged
the fair cheek of Mrs. Preston. The lackey
moved off to the door with great deliberation,
as he always did when he had, so to speak, the
credit of his master or mistress buttoned up in

his pocket. It took from the menial and added to the dignity of the man when he was conscious, as he often was, of being a pillar for the support of the respectability of the family. His air was more clerical than usual when he opened the street-door, prepared to encounter Mrs. Brace, who was well known to him.

Instead of that lady there stood upon the highest of the brown-stone steps a burly expressman, with a shabby little trunk upon his shoulder, tied together with a cord.

" This is for here, my cove," said the man, bluntly; "and there's forty cents due."

This low familiarity of address was offensive to Robert's nostrils. " You've made a mistake," said he, loftily. " There's no such trunk expected at this house."

" I haint made no mistake, nuther, now, you popinjay. I guess I've got the company's credit to take care of; and here's the number in my check book—92 West —— street, as plain as black and white can make it."

Then it goes to the servants' door," replied Robert, trying hard to keep up a show of dignity, as he saw the expressman was an ugly customer when roused, and had a formidable pair of fists. "It may possibly belong to the new cook."

"I don't care a flip who it belongs to. If it goes down to the servants' door it goes down on a pair of shoulders about the size of your'n. Here I stays until I gets my pay."

He pushed into the vestibule, and set the trunk down on the marble tiling with a bang.

Mrs. Preston had heard loud voices in the hall, and felt a rush of cold air from the open door with certain inward quakings. She thought she recognized the tones of Madame Pulsifer's young man, who was very obstinate, as she well knew from sad experience. To-day Robert must fight her battle for her. She got up and moved round the elegant drawing-room guiltily, waiting to hear the front door close and the disagreeable sounds die away. Her restlessness chanced to lead her to the window ; and, as she glanced through the heavy draperies of lace and satin, her eye happened to light upon the express wagon standing there in front of the house loaded with trunks. Immediately came the thought that she had made a mistake, and with it an immense sense of relief. She stepped at once into the hall.

"What is all this noise about, Robert?"

. "Indeed, ma'am, here's a fellow determined to leave a trunk that don't belong to the house."

"How, pray, do you know it don't belong to the house?"

Robert had only judged from the lights he possessed. "I've never seen the likes of it coming to the house before."

"Here's the number, mum, on the company's check, and I'll be blowed if I'll budge an inch till I gets my pay."

"I dare say it's all right," said Mrs. Preston pleasantly, with an inward conviction that soft words do sometimes butter parsnips. "I am not looking for any one from a distance, but an unexpected visitor might arrive. Just do me the favor to look at the name on the trunk, if there is one, and I think I can tell if it is to come to this house."

The man, who had coolly sat down on the offending trunk, got on his pegs and jerked up the shabby little affair on end, and looked at the name, written in a cramped, old-fashioned hand on a business card:

"Mrs. Hannah Thorburn, Plastow."

" Mrs. Thorburn, of course ; my husband's great aunt. Robert, you should not be so forth-putting. It would have been more becoming in you to have made inquiries."

" Indeed, ma'am, I thought I had warrant."

" You had no warrant to take any such matter upon yourself."

Mrs. Preston satisfied the expressman, and ordered Robert, who was huffy, to carry the shabby little black trunk, much frayed at the corners, up to the third-story back room.

As Robert bent his aristocratic shoulders to the obnoxious burden, he determined to give warning before the end of the month. The Prestons did not come up to his idea of a genteel family.

The elegant little mistress herself, who was not quite as fastidious as Robert, felt half ashamed at not having assigned Aunt Thorburn to the best guest-chamber. She knew her husband honored and loved this aunt ; she had often heard him speak of her goodness to him when he was a poor boy up in Plastow. Still, she reflected that Aunt Thorburn was not used to any thing half so fine as the third-story back room ; and, perhaps, she would be more at her ease there than in the grander apartment down stairs.

While these thoughts were running through her head the relative from Plastow was ushered in. She was a tall, almost gaunt, woman, with rather an unyielding countenance, bordered by gray hair quite guiltless of dye. Her bonnet was at least five seasons behind the fashion, and she wore over her black alpaca dress a black-and-white shawl of the species known as Bay State.

Mrs. Preston's greeting was very gracious indeed. She had a little innocent design upon Aunt Thorburn, and meant to dazzle her a good deal, and perhaps to awe her the least bit in the world. But the country aunt was a quiet, unmoved sort of body; and, whatever she may have felt underneath, she did not appear to be overcome by the magnificence of her nephew's residence or the stylishness of his little wife. But there are one or two facts that prove to my mind that Aunt Thorburn was really cowed; she called Robert sir; and when she got to her own room, and was left to adjust herself as best she could to its new-fangled knickknackeries, she spread her handkerchief over the seat of the crimson satin sofa before she ventured to sit down and rest.

The lunch-bell tingled, and she made her way down stairs again, feeling very much like a cat in a strange garret, after opening several wrong doors and walking surreptitiously into two or three pantries. Mrs. Preston was in the parlor with the children—three little girls, the youngest a mere toddler—with faces clustering like dewy rose-buds against mamma's skirts, their white frocks set off by bright sashes and shoulder-knots. Aunt Thorburn's visage looked much less unyielding than it had done as she stooped down to kiss them, and lay her large, bony hand on their tender little heads. She really was gaunter and plainer than she had appeared in her wraps. Her rather skimpy black dress fell round her in stiff lines. There was no hint of a waterfall in the arrangement of her hair. Scant and gray as it was, it was wadded in a small knot under her half-cap of cheap lace, trimmed with lappets of rusty black velvet. Her linen collar was fastened with an antiquated mourning pin, and her cuffs, of the same material, did not seem to be on the best of terms with her large red wrists.

Miss Lu Edgecombe, Mrs. Preston's sister, dropped in to lunch. She was a lively girl, arrayed in a medley of garnet and black silk, that broke out all over her in puffs and coils and tags and fringes. Her bonnet was composed of five green leaves, with nothing visible to hold it on to a sea of blonde hair, that raged down her back in waves and over her forehead in ripples. She wore lavender gloves, three buttons, and carried a dainty white parasol covered with point.

Aunt Thorburn had probably heard of this extraordinary species of young creature; but, having never come across a good specimen before, she was excusable for staring a little through her specs.

"Who under the sun have you got now, Clara?" whispered Lu, dragging her sister into the hall.

"Henry's Aunt Thorburn. You must have heard of her. He is always boasting about her mince-pies and cider-apple sauce."

"That's just like Frank." (Frank was at present Lu's slave—soon to become her lord.) "You know he was a country boy, too. Nothing ever tastes to him as the dishes his mother

used to cook. I expect to have the old lady
held up daily as a warning and admonition after
I get to housekeeping.

" Henry thinks the world of this old aunt."

" She isn't a fascinator, is she, Clara ? "

" No ; of course not. Every body can't be
fascinators."

"But she might get herself up to look a
little less as if she had just stepped out of the
ark."

" That's a fact. She must have means ; for
I remember Henry said her husband, the
Deacon, left her a farm and some money in the
bank."

" I'm rather sorry she has turned up just
now. There's Beth's wedding coming off next
week, and I thought of bringing the Greshams
over to-night, to pass a social evening."

" You had better not. Henry will want to
talk over old times with his aunt. We must be
polite to her whatever happens."

" You will have to do New York for her
benefit, I suppose. Imagine yourself mounting
up to the top of Trinity steeple, and pointing
out the beauties of the Battery and the City
Hall."

"Barnum's is burnt up, at any rate," said Mrs. Preston, laughingly. "That is so much in my favor."

"Well, then," after a little pause, "I suppose I can't have the carriage to-morrow to pay calls with."

"No, I am afraid not."

Miss Lu was just taking her leave, when Aunt Thorburn entered with the little girls. She had coaxed them to get acquainted by some freemasonry of her own, and now they were all jabbering at once. Lu had her hand on the knob when the bell rang. Mrs. Preston, who was still in bondage to the dread of Madame Pulsifer's young man, had no time to adopt a line of policy before the door opened, and exposed to view a boy—a tall, weak-looking lad—dressed in poor clothes much too small for him, with hollow, bloodless cheeks, that certainly gave no sign of gormandizing.

"O, it's Johnny Spencer. Come in, Johnny. How is your mother to-day?"

Johnny came in and pulled off his cap.

"Thank you, ma'am, I'm sorry to say she's poorly again. Last week she had one of her bad turns. The doctor said she took cold holding her arms out of bed ; but you see, ma'am, she had these yokes to finish, and she could not afford to lie idle."

"I am sorry she hurried on my account," said Mrs. Preston kindly, taking the little newspaper parcel from the lad's hand. "There are two more up stairs she shall have ; but tell her to take her own time, and not to worry over them a bit."

"Indeed, ma'am, I wish she could take her time. I'm afraid it will kill her to keep on so."

"And why can't she, Johnny ?"

"O, ma'am, there's bread and medicine and coal to buy, and the rent coming due regular every month, and I not big enough to help her much."

"O, yes, of course ; I know all that. You are a good boy to your mother, if there ever was one. Now go down stairs, and I will tell the cook to put you up some tea and sugar."

"Thank you kindly, ma'am." The lad hesitated and twisted his cap, and a tinge of color came into his hollow cheek. "But, if you please, ma'am, mother said she would like to get her pay."

"Wont to-morrow morning do as well,

Johnny? I really haven't the sum about me. It don't often happen so; but Mr. Preston could not give me any money this morning. He said he would bring it up to-night."

Johnny twisted his cap more persistently than ever, and the color rose in the hollow of his cheek; but he stood his ground. "I'm afraid it wouldn't do, ma'am. You see the money was borrowed, and we promised to have it ready this evening."

"Dear, dear! I am very sorry. Lu," (to her sister, who had turned back to examine the yokes,) "couldn't you lend me five dollars?"

"No; really, Clara, I am a little short myself to-day. But you don't pretend to say that you got this work done for five dollars a pair? I never knew any thing so cheap in my life."

Mrs. Preston did not heed her sister's remark. She was casting about in her thoughts to see what could be done for Johnny.

"I can let you have five dollars as well as not," said Aunt Thorburn, coming in like a good Providence at the right moment.

"O, could you? It would oblige me immensely."

Aunt Thorburn pulled her long, old-fashioned bead purse from the depths of her pocket.

"What did you say ailed your ma, bub?" she asked Johnny as she was extricating the bills.

" She has retching, ma'am, and a holler pain in her side, and an all-goneness, and hot flashes like."

" I know what that hollow pain is ; I've had it myself often. You tell her to soak her feet before she goes to bed, and lay on a bag of warm hops."

Johnny said he would be sure and remember.

"I'm coming to see your ma," whispered Aunt Thorburn as she slipped an extra fifty cents into the lad's hand, and sent him off as happy as a king.

Mrs. Preston's handsome turnout stood aa the door, ready to take her to the Park. Of course, Aunt Thorburn was asked to go along ; although Mrs. Preston almost hoped she would plead a headache, or the fatigue of her journey, as an excuse for staying quietly at home. She did not appreciate the fact that a four hours' ride in the rail-cars, on a bright autumn morning, was mere child's play compared with what Aunt

Thorburn did every day of her life at home, up in Plastow.

The old lady came down arrayed in the same antiquated bonnet and blanket shawl that had served her for a traveling costume. Mrs. Preston had her own pet prejudices, and one of them happened to be a strong dislike for a shawl of this particular description. However, the obnoxious garment lay pressed against her own rich velvet and lace on the back seat of the open barouche, while the little girls sat in front, and made the air musical with their pretty prattle.

It was one of the perfect afternoons at the Park. The foliage of the Ramble was just tinged with autumnal hues, the near city looked transfigured through a violet haze, the pretty bridges were crowded with pleasure-seekers, the swans swam off proudly through the lucent water of the lake, and the bright green Common was dotted over with the sheep. Terrace Bridge, with its floating banners and gay boatloads, looked like a glimpse from some fair Venetian picture.

Aunt Thorburn knew it "beat" any thing up at Plastow "all hollow;" but she was a little afraid of appearing countryfied and admiring the wrong things, so she did not give expression to quite all she felt. However, on driving home through Fifth Avenue, with a crowd of fine carriages and prancing steeds, while the blue haze of early dusk filled the beautiful street, and the clear, sweet sunset just rosed the tops of the highest houses, and the gas-lamps began to flicker down Murray Hill, like golden blossoms on invisible stems, Aunt Thorburn's face did relax to an expression of unmixed enjoyment.

I am afraid Mrs. Preston was not perfectly satisfied with her drive. She had met a number of fashionable acquaintances, and every nod or smile of recognition from a passing carriage awoke a disagreeable consciousness of that horrid old blanket shawl by her side. Mrs. Preston was right, nevertheless, in thinking her husband would be glad to see his old relative. He was right glad to see her, much to his credit, be it said. He took her two old bony hands in his, and kissed her rather hard-looking cheek in the heartiest fashion.

"Where have you put Aunt?" he asked after a while of his wife.

"Up in the third story, Henry. I thought she would be more quiet and retired up there."

Mr. Preston knit his brow. "You ought to remember, Clara," said he, coldly, "that Aunt is not as young as we are, and how un-accustomed she is to climbing the stairs of a city house. You had better tell Robert to bring her things down into the room on the second floor, and kindle a little fire in the grate to take off the chill."

The entire evening was spent in talking over old times. Mrs. Preston thought this species of entertainment slow and stupid; but her husband enjoyed it hugely. His early days were certainly not very distinguished, as he had begun life a poor boy and worked his own way up to wealth and an enviable position on 'Change. Still he dearly loved to go back to them, and live over the "scrapes" and madcap adventures of those humble times.

He was in high good humor when he got to his room that night, after saying all the cheery last things he could think of to his old relative. He had made a snug little sum of money during the day on the rise of his favorite stock.

"I ran into Ball & Black's, Clara," said he,

"as I was passing to-night, and these trinkets took my eye. Pretty, now, aint they?"

"O lovely!" cried Mrs. Preston, holding up a pair of exquisite pearl ear-rings. "And for me, of course?"

"Certainly. Who else should a fellow like me buy ear-rings for but his wife?"

"You are the best husband I ever had!" And Mrs. Preston, in her gratitude, got very close to him, and hid her rosy little mouth in his mustache. "But, dear," she changed her tone slightly, "did you bring that cheek you promised?"

"O bother the check! What a beggar you are, Clara."

"I know it, but what can I do? Here, to-night, has come in a large bill for children's shoes."

"Bills, bills! Confound bills! I hate the word."

"We can't dispense with the thing, though. To-day I was actually penniless, and found my-self reduced to the necessity of borrowing from your aunt."

"Borrowing from my aunt!"

"She happened to be in the hall when Johnny

Spencer came. His mother has been doing some needlework for me. She is sick, and in want of the money ; so your aunt offered to pay."

"That was awkward—deuced awkward! How much do you want?" The question was put in a very icy tone.

"I must have at least a hundred, Henry. I owe Madame Pulsifer alone almost that sum."

Mr. Preston sniffed at the name. "It does appear to me, Clara, that you will have to retrench in your personal expenses."

Mrs. Preston had heard the same thing before. If there were any two words in the English language she hated, they were "retrench" and "curtail." The pair went to rest that night, in their splendid home, with a cloud between them. But next morning's brilliant sun scattered it into nothingness, and shrewd little Mrs. Clara prepared to put into execution a plan she had formed over night.

"I suppose you would like to do some shopping, wouldn't you, Aunt? The horses are at the door, and I can drive you to Stewart's as well as not."

Aunt Thorburn had two of the little girls in

her lap. She was telling them the absorbing history of her calf, Spot ; but she broke off immediately, and looked up through her specs at Mrs. Preston.

"Shopping! That's what we call trading, I 'spose. I don't know as I'm in want of any thing in particular for myself. I did calculate on buying some things for Elviry. She's my niece that used to live with me. Her husband hain't no faculty for getting along. There isn't much to live on, and a big family of children to feed and clothe. I don't allow you'll feel much interested in her, though. I should like to take a squint at Stewart's gret store, but there's no hurry at all."

"Wouldn't you like to get a nice winter cloak for yourself, Aunt? I saw some at Stewart's the other day that I am sure would suit you exactly, and they struck me as very cheap."

"How much be they ?"

"Eighty dollars."

"Eighty dollars!" repeated Aunt Thorburn slowly. "I can't begin to afford it."

Of course, nothing more was said about the cloak ; but Mrs. Preston set it down in her own mind that Aunt Thorburn was close and penurious. She had no very near relative to save her money for, and it did seem strange she could not afford to dress respectably. The old blanket shawl seemed more of a grievance than ever, and Mrs. Preston felt inwardly irritated every time it came in contact with her own rich raiment.

"Didn't you tell me, Henry," she said to her husband, when opportunity offered, "that your Aunt Thorburn was well off?"

"Well off, certainly, for the country. The term means something quite different up in Plastow from what it does here in New York."

"I do wish she would get some new clothes, and fix up a little while she is here in the city."

"I haven't noticed any thing amiss with her. She always looks good to me whatever she has on." Mr. Preston spoke with a slight degree of acerbity. He never encouraged criticism on his own side of the house.

Mrs. Preston dropped the subject for the present, but she was more and more convinced that Aunt Thorburn was niggardly. When Sunday came, the little lady had hoped her husband would propose to take his relative over to Brooklyn, to hear a certain celebrated preacher who does not hold forth strictly to an upper-ten audience. Now Mrs. Preston's church was an upper-ten church, and all the worshipers round about her pew knew the cost of her camel's hair shawl and the exact value of her diamonds.

However, with a contrariness not uncommon to men, Mr. Preston said, although he had no warrant for saying it, that his aunt was going to stay a number of weeks, and there would be plenty of time for Brooklyn ; he wanted her to hear his own minister first. Accordingly, the camel's hair shawl went into the house of God alongside the old black-and-white plaid ; and I am afraid Mrs. Preston thought more about that and about Aunt Thorburn's stinginess than she did of the sermon, which was on the danger of growing worldly.

" I will take you this afternoon anywhere you would like to go," said Mrs. Preston to Aunt Thorburn after dinner was over, and Mr. Preston had stretched himself out on the sofa for a Sunday nap.

" Well, now," returned the old lady, " I

should like to visit the Five Points (she pronounced it Pints) House of Industry ; but I
dare say you've been there so often it wouldn't
be any treat to you."

Mrs. Preston was feign to confess, with a
degree of shame, that she had never visited that
excellent institution, but she declared herself
quite ready to go. She put on her plainest
walking-suit and her shabbiest bonnet, and they
set off in the horse-car.

I will not attempt to describe that most
touching sight—a congregation of poor, de-
graded little beings, picked up and gathered in
from the streets to listen to good words and
feel the touch of a blessed human charity.

Mrs. Preston had a mother's heart in her
bosom, and she sat and cried softly behind her
thread-lace vail all through the exercises.

When they were over, Aunt Thorburn made
her way to the superintendent and slipped a
little roll of bills into his hand. He looked at it
in surprise.

"A hundred dollars ! What name did you
say ?"

"Hannah Thorburn, from Plastow."

"Mrs. Thorburn, I do not know how to

express my thanks for so generous a gift. It comes just when it is most needed."

Aunt Thorburn made her escape. A hundred dollars! Had Mrs. Preston heard aright? She had given a dollar herself; it was all she thought she could afford. When they got into the street, while the tears were still wet upon her cheeks, she asked the question.

"Well, yes," said Aunt Thorburn. "You see there aint many chances of doing good up in Plastow. The farmers are all pretty forehanded in our community."

Not many chances of doing good! Mrs. Preston did not speak again for some time. She was feeling sorry for her harsh judgment of Aunt Thorburn—for calling her stingy and mean in her thoughts. She was feeling, too, as if she would like to take up a corner of the old black-and-white shawl and kiss it.

Aunt Thorburn did stay in New York several weeks. She saw Johnny and his mother, and comforted them. She filled all the spare corners of her shabby little trunk with things for Elvira and the children. She saw more of the charitable institutions of New York and did more for them in one month than Henry Preston and his wife had done in twelve years. If there is a saint's niche in the Preston family, I think Aunt Thorburn is destined to stand there with her old black-and-white plaid blanket shawl wrapped round her gaunt shoulders; and perhaps her nephew and his wife will look up to the old lady's height, and be helped out of the slough of selfish indulgence, in which they were in great danger of getting mired.

AMOS STANHOPE'S PRACTICAL JOKE.

"NOW, boys, don't hector Lyddy," said Mrs. Stanhope as she untied the tapestrings of her checked apron, and with a little sigh of relief settled into the wicker-backed rocking-chair.

"Of course not," returned Amos, as grave as a judge, while at the same time he gave his brother Sam a private nudge. "But why couldn't she bring her beau right in here, and let us get a squint at him? If father was at home he wouldn't like her to be having an extra fire and light in the keeping-room."

"O it's no great matter," said Mrs. Stanhope, taking up her basket of mending, which always appeared to be in a chronic state of overflow. "We can bring the coals out as soon as Mr. Hardy goes. And you had better not speak about it to father," she added, with a twinge of remorse at the small lessons of deceit she was obliged to instill; "for poor Lyddy don't have many pleasures."

"I guess I know how to hold my tongue," replied Amos, a little sharply, as he smeared out a sum upon his slate with the elbow of his jacket; "but it would be fun to tease Lyddy about the sparking. I should think a fellow would feel awful streaked running after a girl, and sitting up and twirling his thumbs before her. You'll never catch me at that business, see if you do."

" There's no telling what foolishness you may go into one of these days," said Mrs. Stanhope, with a faint smile circling her sad lips. "But come, now, you had better make haste to bed. There is Sam nodding over his book, and I shall have no end of trouble to get you up in the morning in time to do the chores."

Amos lighted his candle rather reluctantly, and began to climb the chamber-stair, with little Sam behind, yawning and carrying his shoes in his hand.

" Suppose we go and listen at the stove-pipe hole," whispered Amos in Sam's ear, with a suppressed chuckle. " It would be such prime fun to hear that spooney's soft speeches."

Sam woke up bright at the prospect of a "lark." And Amos blew out the candle, and in their stocking-feet the boys stole to the spare chamber, and applied their ears to the stove-pipe-hole, pinching each other to keep from " snorting," as Amos expressed it. There was a peculiarly sonorous quality to the voice of Lyddy's beau that brought sound without sense to the roguish listeners ; or else he spoke in a low, confidential tone, which seemed to go on most of the time, except when it was interrupted by Lyddy's pleased, shy little laugh.

Just as Amos had creaked the loose board overhead, and was holding his breath for fear he should be discovered, the outside door closed and Lyddy's beau was gone. The young girl stood a moment in the keeping-room, and heard the runners of his cutter creak as he turned out into the hard-packed road. Mr. Hardy's mare was restive from standing so long in the cold ; and now he let her go as straight as an arrow, shaking off a spray of music from the sleigh-bells. Lyddy's cheeks were burning over something Ben Hardy had done at parting. It was certainly very impertinent in the young man, and she ought to be very angry with him for taking her so completely by surprise. It should never happen again—no, never; and she would keep it a dead secret, locked in her own bosom.

So, still flustered, Lyddy ran out into the kitchen, where her mother sat by the dying embers of the hearth, putting the last patch on Sam's trousers. Lyddy was scarcely a pretty girl, but there was something very soft and feminine about her. The old blue de laine, which had been turned twice in the skirt, and would have looked like a fright on any body else, seemed to make a perfect toilet for Lyddy as she settled down in its folds at her mother's feet, with the red, uncertain light from the coals on the hearth playing over her fleecy hair and reddening her delicate cheek, which was not plump enough to give evidence of buxom health.

Mrs. Stanhope was tall, gaunt, and bony, with marks of toil and anxiety upon her bent shoulders and gray, joyless face, where the blanching locks were smoothed back in perfect plainness. It was easy to see that she had never had, even in her youth, the soft, round outlines of Lyddy's form; but there was an exceeding tenderness in her face as it beamed on her young daughter, which seemed to glorify the rugged features. You saw that Lyddy was the apple of her eye —the white dove that folded its wings in her careworn bosom-—the ewe lamb she would wish to bear in her arms over all the rough places of the world.

The old kitchen, with its low walls and heavy beams, was very much in shadow now, except the red core of the fire, and Lyddy sitting by it, against the background made by her mother's chair.

" Wasn't it odd Mr. Hardy should have come all the way over from Millford just to call?" said Lyddy, pulling down Mrs. Stanhope's hand from the coarse mending, and patting the big steel thimble on the middle finger, and the hard joints, enlarged by hard work. " His father is the rich man up at Millford, a merchant and mill-owner ; and all the girls are crazy after Ben."

Mrs. Stanhope smiled a sad, wistful sort of smile, and it seemed to her that she was about to get a glimpse into the depths of Lyddy's simple, unsullied heart.

"I hope Mr. Hardy is a young man of good habits and principles," said she, " Rich men's sons are too apt to depend on their father's money. I don't want any body to come after you, Lyddy, who can't make his own way in the world."

" Of course, mother, he don't mean any thing. That is—I don't believe Ben has got a bad habit in the world, unless he is fond of tobacco. The young men of Millford are a hard set, and go on sprees sometimes ; but Ben has always kept clear of them. He says a man must respect himself first, if he is going to come to anything in life. You ought to hear him talk, mother. He is going out West for a year to get established in business."

Lyddy's cheeks were burning again, and her little warm hands were nervously fumbling Mrs. Stanhope's. The grave, sad-eyed woman smiled again with a feeling half sweet, half pathetic, and seemed to glance far back to a day in her own life when there was a faintly-budding romance, which had soon withered and died.

"You must be very careful, Lyddy. It's a serious thing to get to thinking too much about a person. Folks marry sometimes when they are quite ignorant of their own hearts, and wake up to find they have made a mistake."

"O, mother, don't be so doleful!" cried
Lyddy. "There isn't any thing between Ben
and me. I don't believe he means much!" and
her voice died out faintly, and her heart gave a
dull thud, with the consciousness that it would
be very dreary if Ben didn't mean much. "I
thought it would be so nice," she went on, "if
we could have the girls in some evening before
Ben goes way. Father wont be home until
next week, and he need not know a word about
it. You know, mother, I never do have company at home, and I feel ashamed to go anywhere on that account."

"I don't know what your father would say,
Lyddy, if he should hear we had been getting
up a party in his absence. The girls might
seem to happen in, though, might they not? I
could send a pail of butter over to the store by
Amos to buy loaf sugar for a cake, and we have
got apples and hickory-nuts and cider enough
in the house to help along ; and I think just this
once I might squeeze out a cup of coffee."

Mrs. Stanhope hated the small deceptions
she was obliged to practice in her family; and,
with a serious and reflective turn of mind, she
dreaded the consequences upon her children.

The next morning, when she gave the pail of butter to Amos, and charged him with a secret mission to the store-keeper, the boy flared up.

"Mother," said he, "in a year or two I'm going to quit the old shanty, and then I guess I can earn money enough to keep you above board, so that you wont have to pinch and screw. I do hate this underhand business like poison."

"Amos, don't speak of your home in that way."

"I can't help it, when, to tell the truth, father is so tight he wont let us have things like other folks. How can he expect us to be fond of home, I should like to know?"

"Hush, child! Your father is an industrious, sober, hard-working man, and does what he thinks is right. Remember what the Bible says about honoring your parents, and how much worse it would be if he was a drunkard."

The faults which people happen to be free from do not excuse those they have. Amos trudged away quite unconvinced by this logic, and thinking what a change he would make in his life when he should acquire the rights of a man.

There was happiness enough for Mrs. Stan-

hope in watching Lyddy as she tripped about
the old dilapidated farm-house, inventing little
feminine contrivances to make the dingy rooms
look a thought more cheery. The faded chintz
lounge-cover was washed and starched fresh,
and the holes in the carpet mended with patches
of the same. Lyddy placed the furniture about
so as skillfully to hide the worn spots. Good,
neighborly Mrs. Shaw lent her plated candle-
sticks and high preserve dishes ; and Lyddy,
while she rubbed the knives and got little smears
of brickdust on her pretty round arms, was all
the time whispering to herself that she wasn't
the least bit in love with Ben Hardy.

She was a good deal puzzled to know just
how to word her note of invitation ; and at last
opened it in a very prim, school-ma'amish way,
which Ben did not imitate in his reply. He
began, " Dearest Lyddy," as natural as you
please ; and the foolish, fond little girl kissed
the words in a flutter of delight, and hid the
billet in her bosom.

It is not probable that Mrs. Stanhope would
have ventured into the room at all that evening
if her curiosity concerning " Lyddy's beau " had
not been excessive. She thought her place was

in the kitchen, making the coffee and setting out the best blue dishes ; but Lyddy would have her put on her Sunday gown, and hide her scant gray hair under a cappy head-dress, which she had made out of the trimmings of her last summer's bonnet and an old lace vail, come down, as Lyddy remarked, from the year one.

"It's so long since I've been in company," said Mrs. Stanhope, in a good deal of a fluster, " I'm afraid I sha'n't know how to appear."

" Never mind, mother," said Lyddy, capering about her, and adding the last touches to her dress. "We'll have you as lively as a cricket before the evening is over."

Lyddy's soft cheeks were blooming, and her eyes were bright and moist with pleasant excitement. She wore her old dove-colored parametta, with three darns on the back breadth ; but the blue neck-ribbon and the smiling face of the little maiden seemed to glorify it.

"We must be careful of the loaf sugar, and not cut any more cake than will be needed. For my part I don't care for cake," said Mrs. Stanhope, with the wrinkles of the careful Martha forming between her eyebrows.

"Whew! I guess I do!" put in Amos, who

was dressing in one corner of the room. "I'll have as much as I can eat for once in my life. Hang it! these collars never will set anyhow," and he gave his cravat an angry jerk. "Do, Lyddy, come and see if you can't tie a decent bow."

"You will behave yourself like a gentleman to-night, wont you, Amos, and not be up to any pranks?" coaxed Lyddy as she fussed about the boy's neck with her slender fingers, and clipped the ragged part from his collar, and tied his bow to a charm.

"I guess I shall keep a little shady," returned Amos; "for my shoes have got two great cracks in them, and I hate the girls like poison. They are always making fun of a fellow. What I go in for is the good eating."

Three large sleigh-loads of merry-makers drove up to the door in the sparkling winter starlight, and stout Miss Brewer had to be helped upon her feet by two young men, and, in a weakening fit of laughter, she fell into the arms of a third. This one proved to be Ben Hardy. He freed himself from the armful as soon as he conveniently could, and went to find Lyddy, and to whisper something in her ear which made the lids droop over her eyes and her cheeks flush into sensitive beauty. After that she owned to herself, with a thrill of exquisite joy, that Ben did like her a little ; and, moreover, he was not in the least ashamed to show his partiality.

Amos watched proceedings with the eye of a cynic.

" Pugh ! " He wondered how a fellow could make himself so " soft."

Mrs. Stanhope watched too, with tender and anxious solicitude, and her heart instinctively warmed toward the frank, manly young fellow who could carry on his wooing so bravely. There was Patty Frisbee, a little maiden with snapping black eyes and an active spirit of mischief. Somebody had let her hair down and put a boy's cap on her head, and she was going through the contortions of " Queen Dido."

" Let's have forfeits, or pillows and keys," suggested Bruce Hoyt. Forfeits carried the day, and the very first time Amos was caught tripping, and was judged to "go to Rome," a doom he escaped by making a rush for the door, and slipping through the hands of half a dozen laughing maidens.

"Whew!" thought he as he got outside in the cold air. "I'd sooner take an emetic than go through that job."

After that Ben Hardy was condemned to measure a yard of tape with every girl in the room, and he went about the business with commendable alacrity. Miss Brewer took refuge behind a rocking-chair, and rashly declared that nobody should reach her lips; but the young man boldly scaled the barrier, and the business of tape-measuring went on amid a series of little hysterical screams and much disarrangement of the lady's back hair. When he came to Lyddy's place, she had vanished; and Ben, who was keen on the scent, having done so much lip-service to reach her, was obliged to pursue into unknown regions—the kitchen, and even the wood-shed—where, it is to be supposed, he took ample revenge for his pains.

Then there followed a round game; and Ben Hardy actually pulled Mrs. Stanhope into the play, and made her spin about like a top.

"Do let me ketch a breath," gasped the good woman, sinking down into a chair, weak and exhausted with laughter. "I'm clean beat out, and any body would think I was fit for an asylum."

When it came to the guessing plays, Amos and Patty Frisbee were sent out into the entry. By this time they had about come to the con- clusion that they were affinities. Patty had a boy's tastes, and liked fun; and there was no stuff and nonsense about her. The two were just ripe for mischief. Mr. Hardy's coat —a very nice new one, with velvet collar and frogged buttons—was hanging on a nail in the entry.

"What a swell that chap is!" said Amos, pulling out one end of a white handkerchief from the pocket. "Pugh! it smells like a drug-shop."

"There's something heavy in the tail-pocket," returned Patty. "Would you mind putting in your hand to feel it?"

Amos followed the roguish girl's suggestion, and pulled out a handsome tobacco-box, lined with tortoise-shell.

"Wouldn't it be fun to fill it with pepper?" whispered Patty.

"No. Soft-soap would do better," returned Amos, who was apt to carry things too far.

"I could make him think Lyddy did it," added Patty, "and that would be a splendid joke."

Before the call came from the keeping-room the boy had filled Mr. Hardy's box with a very dark, soft substance, and slipped it back into its place. During the remainder of the evening Amos and Patty exploded in a burst of merriment whenever they chanced to meet.

"What's the joke?" inquired Mr. Hardy as he chased the madcap round the room in a game of fox and geese.

"Ask Lyddy," replied Patty, her eyes dancing with mischief. "She knows all about it." And poor Lyddy, to keep the fun going, pretended she did know, when, in truth, she was as unconscious as an infant.

That night Lyddy went to bed wondering if she should ever pass another evening so full of happiness as this had been. She hid her face in the pillow with delicious and confusing memories of Mr. Hardy, and then a fit of humility came upon her, and she wondered how he could care for a simple, plain little girl like her. She could not think of the future, so content was she with the blissful, inexplicable present.

Amos, when opportunity allowed him to re-
flect on his practical joke, grew half ashamed of
himself and apprehensive of consequences. He
longed to make a clean breast of it to Lyddy,
for there was nothing ungenerous or sneaking
in the lad's nature; but he was hurried with
his chores in the morning, and after that was
obliged to make haste to school, so that poor
Lyddy was left in utter ignorance of the evil
impending. At noon there came a note from
Millford. Lyddy knew Ben's handwriting, and
she ran with it to her chamber and kissed
it foolishly and fondly over and over again.
It seemed as though every thing must have
stood still for a moment when Lyddy opened
the little billet and her eyes fell upon the first
words. It began :

"Miss Stanhope, I feel that I was grossly in-
sulted in your house last night, and it gives
me the greatest pain to believe that you were
aware of the circumstances. The pockets of
my great-coat were meddled with, and my tobacco-box was maliciously filled with soft-soap,
which, when the box was carelessly opened, ran
down upon my clothes and utterly ruined them.

The loss is of small consequence, but the indignity I deeply feel. I had heretofore flattered myself that you were my friend, but this occurrence puts things in a new light.

(Signed) "B. HARDY."

The note was written by an angry man, who would certainly one day repent of his anger; but no consideration of this kind softened the heavy blow which Lyddy was called upon to sustain. When Amos got home at night he found her face pale, and her eyes red and swollen from weeping. In shame and sorrow of heart the boy confessed his sin. Mrs. Stanhope would not rest until Amos had written a humble, repentant letter to Mr. Hardy, clearing poor Lyddy from every shade of blame.

Spring had come, and it seemed to Lyddy that the thread of her pretty romance had been snapped asunder, never again to be mended. Her face grew shadowy, wan, and wistful; but she did not complain. Ben Hardy had not come back. She knew that he had left Millford, and probably long before this time he had forgotten the little, loving, confiding girl whose heart he had so surely won, for Lyddy did not deceive herself any longer. She sighed, and went about her work, and tried to forget— a task she never could accomplish.

Mrs. Stanhope had been sick with a low fever for many weeks, and a hired girl was not to be thought of in Mrs. Stanhope's economy, so the brunt of the work fell upon Lyddy's shoulders. She did not mind it much. She was glad to have something to fill her hands full. But every day the little face grew more spiritual, sweet, and patient; and the sick mother, following her child's motions with large, bright eyes, seemed to be always praying. A great change had come over Amos. He seemed to have outgrown the boorish, unmanly pranks of a boy, and, with the thoughtful kindness of a man, to try and make Lyddy forget the wrong he had done her.

One spring day, when the orchards were like soft, rosy clouds resting upon the earth, Lyddy went out to breathe the fresh air, and walked along the perfumed roads, and pressed the tender young grass, and thought it would not be very hard to die, even when every thing was in its first budding beauty. Just as she had reached Bright's Corner, and was turning back toward home, a horseman came spurring round the turn. Instantly he sprang to the ground, and seized both of Lyddy's little trembling hands in his. It was Ben Hardy, looking browner and handsomer and more irresistible than ever. Lyddy afterward could not remember just what happened ; but there seemed to be a happy mist about her, and Ben was saying something over and over again in a very tender and thrilling tone.

"Can you forgive me, Lyddy, for that cruel, savage note? Patty Frisbee made me believe you had a hand in the joke, and Amos's letter miscarried, and followed me all over the West. But before I knew the truth my heart was so sick with longing to see you, and make it up, I was heartily ashamed of myself, and only wanted an excuse to come back."

"I hope you have forgiven poor Amos," said Lyddy, hardly knowing what words were shaping themselves upon her lips. "He has been so miserable and low-spirited about it."

"Forgiven him!" cried Ben. "He is a capital fellow, and has done me a real service. His prank so disgusted me with tobacco in all its forms I have never been able to touch it since, and within the last six months I have more than saved the price of a new suit of clothes, better than those that were spoiled."

Within two years after Lyddy's marriage Amos wrote a love-letter to Patty Frisbee, which she showed to all the girls and made no end of fun of. He is still unmarried. The firm of Hardy & Stanhope now does a flourishing business out West, and old Mrs. Stanhope looks younger and happier than she did ten years ago. Her children have made her life soft and easy; and the old farm-house wears a look of comfort and plenty, which it never wore in the days when Lyddy was a girl.

THE OLD SQUIRE'S WRATH.

———◆———

THE gates of the old Northrup place stood wide open—which was their usual attitude —and the house wore a warm, comfortable, low-browed look, in spite of the gaunt trees behind it, and the bleak November sky, betokening snow. It was a sort of eye-brightener to the chilled farmers driving past with loads of cheese-boxes or starkly-frozen pork. Sometimes one or another would point out the old place with his whip to some chance companion on the seat beside him, and then would come the question:

"Is the old Squire alive yet?"

"Bless you, yes; and as brisk as he was at forty, and as straight as an elum-sapling. The Squire is reg'lar old style, brass-mounted. You heard, didn't you, how he turned his girl out of doors long ago for marrying against his wishes? He's never given in a hair. Folks in these parts call him a pretty hard old customer,"

And sometimes, in the rattle of wagon-wheels over the frozen ruts, the two last syllables of the epithet appeared to be dispensed with.

Jerry, the clock-mender and licensed stroller of the country side, was coming out of Squire Northrup's door into the nipping cold. His thin old coat, much whitened across the shoulder-blades, and bravely fastened over the chest by two stout pins—for buttons it had none—and his bony, red wrists, and lean shanks, cased though they were in blue yarn socks and a pair of shabby high-lows, promised ill for a long pull in the teeth of the bitter wind. However, Jerry's blue eyes twinkled merrily in his rheumy old face, above many folds of a plaid gingham muffler, for he was conscious of a thanksgiving spare-rib in his kit-bag, and a bottle of Dame Northrup's best cherry bounce, warming, comfortable stuff to a stomach habitually as cold and pinched as was the clock-mender's.

The Squire's wife came trotting out behind, with her cap-strings dabbled in flour and specks of the same powdering her nose. A spicy, mince-meaty fragrance appeared to cling to her big motherly apron ; and her expression, which was habitually " flustercated," as Betsy Bingle,

" the help," expressed it, seemed aggravated by the exigences of the season. There she stood, peering up through her glasses at Jerry, while he raised his hand and hemmed mysteriously.

" It's all right, mum," said he in a loud whisper. " The tin bucket is at the usual roundivoos in the hay-loft, and the things come good to Lindy, I can tell you they did."

" Would it be much out of your way to go home by Batesville ? "

" Not a mite, Miss Northrup. What does a mile or two extra signify to a man when his legs are as sound as the day he was born ! " And Jerry patted his lean nether limbs, as if he considered them a particularly fine pair.

" Then you may stop and tell her the Squire's away from home. I have reckoned it over and over again, and he can't get back till Saturday. It's all along of that jury business, you see ; and, if Lindy chooses to come over with the children on Thanksgiving day, who's to hender ? " inquired the dame, with the anxious wrinkles deepening in her forehead.

There came the sound of a pair of pegged shoes hobbling over the hard path, and Jerry darted off through the shed, and loped away

across country as the bee flies. The dame
gave a guilty little start, and turned around, to
find herself face to face with an old crone, much
bent in body, with bright black eyes peering
out from a scoop bonnet, and the bulge of a
basket showing under a camlet cloak.

"Sakes alive! it's Goody Hinman," said she
briskly, feigning a welcome she scarcely felt;
"and the cold darting like pins and needles.   I
didn't look for you to-day, Goody," she added,
opening the house-door, "but your thanksgiving turkey is ready all the same."

"Don't talk as if I had come a begging, Barberry Ford," responded the old woman sharply,
setting her cane down upon the floor with an
emphatic little thump, "for I mind when you
was nobody but Barberry Ford, a poor sempstress
girl; and folks thought you was doing mighty
well to ketch the Squire with your purty face.
I've come to see the old man," she piped out in
a cracked treble.   "He has hardened his heart
and stiffened his neck, as Scriptur' says; but
Goody Hinman aint afeard of him. They didn't
tell me that Lindy's husband was dead.   They
never do tell the deef old creatur' any thing.
But I found it out; and she left poor, with a

pack of children to keep. Now at Thanksgiving the sons and daughters are coming home to feast and be merry; but there's nobody to think of poor Lindy but old Goody Hinman. You wouldn't have it so, Barberry Ford, if you had a grain of sperit; but the Fords never had the spunk of a louse. I know them all, from Tavern Billy down."

" The Squire has gone from home ! " screamed Dame Northrup, coloring violently and biting her thin lips.

" That's just what I did say," retorted old Goody snappishly, nodding her head as she settled into an easy-chair by the blazing hearth, and let the black scoop fall away from her wide-bordered cap. " The Fords never had the spunk of a louse ; and, if you hadn't knuckled to the old Squire, it might have been better for poor Lindy."

" None so deaf as them that wont hear," murmured the dame, in no pleasant humor, as she stepped back to the table, covered with a maze of butter, and eggs, and spices, and preserve-pots, and flaky pies just rescued from the oven, and others, rarely jiggled and ornamented, standing ready to take their places.

At that moment Betsy Bingle issued from the cellar-way. She was a lean lass, with protruding "shovel" teeth, and a propensity to hold her mouth wide open and listen to every word that was said, to the great detriment of her work, at the same time that she grew singularly limp when she was "beat" or "struck" in her mind, or fell, as she said, into a "quanderary."

Betsy bore in her hand the old lady's thanksgiving turkey, which Goody's sharp eyes no sooner spied than she let fall a live coal she had drawn out from the fire with a pair of tongs to light her short pipe, and seized upon it with avidity.

"It don't heft as much as last year's, not by two pounds," muttered she, ducking and raising the fowl by its long, stiff legs; "and there don't look to be a mossle of fat on the breast-bone."

However, the bird went into Goody's basket, and was carefully covered up with a series of chocolate-tinted cloths; and, scenting pot-pie for dinner with a nose as sharp as her tongue, she settled herself comfortably in her great, roomy, splint-bottomed chair, and let the blue smoke curl in little thin wreaths about her head.

It was the morning of Thanksgiving Day—as Novemberish a morning as you would wish to see, with a bitter wind blowing, and the pale sun wading, as it were, through drifts of snow. The Squire's wife looked out over frost-bitten fields to the edging of timber land, where a few warm colors still burnt like dying embers against a background of evergreens, and then went back from the rating panes to stir the fire into brighter sparkles.

Betsy Bingle was "struck" with the idea that she had never before seen her mistress in such a "twitter," and so long as the handmaid remained in suspense concerning the cause of the flurry she was totally incapable of exertion. Truth to tell, the dame had brisked up wonderfully since the old Squire's departure, from the meeching, timorous, submissive creature she was in his presence. A soft, fluttering rose-color had come into her cheeks, and her eyes looked bright and moist.

Two great turkeys were roasting before the fire, and their unctuous drippings fizzed and sputtered down into the pan. There were loads of good things on the buttery shelves, and the dame was ornamenting the biggest plum-cake with frosting, krissing it, crossing it, dabbing it, and patting it, and quirking her old head this way and that, like an aged robin.

"It's almost time they were here," said she, skipping to the window again, as if she had no more than turned sixteen.

"Do you expect many of 'em?" inquired Betsy, putting in a question at random, and letting some of the egg she was beating slip off into her lap in a little white pool.

"Let me see," said the dame, with her cap turned awry in a very rakish manner, and the specs just ready to fall from the tip of her nose, while she counted upon her knobby old fingers, "One, two, three. Yes, Betsy, there's eight of them."

"My suds!" exclaimed Betsy, "what a raft! You never had more than the parson and his wife, or Deacon Hill's folks."

"Some of them are little teenty-tots," she went on, speaking gleefully, almost as if she had lost Betsy's words; "and to think that I, their grandmother—"

"Stars and garters!" cried Betsy, with a jerk, letting the remaining contents of the platter stream down her dress. "You don't mean to say, Miss Northrup, you've gone and asked your daughter Lindy over to eat thanksgiving dinner?"

"Mind what you are about," said the dame sharply.

"O, luddy! them sillybobs has gone to pot! But I was so beat with the news that I couldn't hold nothing—I never can when I'm scart. Now, Miss Northrup, I wouldn't have thought you'd dast to do it, the old Squire is such a tearer. And who knows but he might pop in unexpected?"

"You let your tongue run too free, Betsy Bingle," said the old lady, bridling a good deal for her; "and you pay too little heed to your work. There, you have spoiled my custards!— all for gabbling about something that don't concern you."

"Mebbe I do gabble," returned Betsy, who was not above answering back. "But I always heard before I come here to live that the old Square's folks was mortal 'fraid of him, and I guess when he hears Lindy's been home he'll make the house hot."

"Go up garret, Betsy," said the dame, quickly

losing sight of her anger in a mingled throng
of memories, poignantly sweet and sad, "and
bring down the two high chairs that belonged
to the twins I lost. I never could bear to see
them around after that. And you may fetch
Lindy's little rocker. The Square brought it
home to her one day from the village, and I
never did see a little creeter so tickled. We
must have a heap of nuts from the store-cham-
ber, Betsy; and the best apples in the cellar—
pearmains and pippins—I recollect Lindy liked
them. And put down a great pitcher of cider
to warm on the hearth, for they'll be chilled to
the marrer in this raw wind."

Betsy clattered off to do her bidding, and the
Squire's wife had just slipped into an old-fashioned, stand-alone silk, and perched a wonderful cap on top of her head, with little gauzy bows
that looked like distracted butterflies, when a
prodigious clatter arose at the door, the cheering of little voices, the thumping of little sturdy
hands and feet. And amid all the din could be
distinguished the cry of " Grandma's house ! "

The dame ran to open it, with an indescribable pucker in her old face, something between
laughing and crying; and there tumbled in a

heap of little sturdy, chubby boys, who had out-
run mother, and the girl-baby, and Jakey, who
had had the rickets and was weak and uncertain in his legs. Grandma made her arms as
wide as she possibly could to take them all in ;
and yet they seemed to spill out and run over,
like rosy-checked apples tumbling from an
apron.

In a moment more a worn woman was standing on the threshold, looking at the first glance
even older than the dame. She wore a shabby
bonnet and thin old shawl, under which peeped
the blue eyes of a very placid baby. No wonder,
remembering how she had gone out from the
old home years before, that Linda should have
broken down and sobbed on her mother's neck.
It seemed to impart a singular and unwonted
degree of courage and strength to the old woman
to see Linda give up—Linda, who had always
been as high-strung and obstinate as the old
Squire himself.

She led her forward to a seat by the warm
fire, and put her feet to toast, and untied the
crumpled bonnet, and let her old hand stray
over the thin hair, turning gray now, and
touched the lined and faded cheek, murmuring

10

soothing words, just as if she had consoled and comforted people all her life long.

Linda's little boys, in spite of their old shoes, that seemed to snicker with funny holes, and the knees of their trowsers patched three deep, and their little taily jackets, made out of old, did not allow any such trifles to damp their spirits. They knew all about grandma's house from their mother's stories, and the awe and mystery surrounding grandpa did not diminish its fascinations. Now it seemed as though a gleesome army of elves had broken into the still old dwelling, and were capering over the wall and cutting didoes on the brown rafters. There was a glorious hubbub, and the bright faces of the geraniums in the sitting-room windows seemed to nod out approvingly at the bleak weather, as much as to say, " This is jolly ; we like it hugely." The little boy who had had the rickets, and couldn't romp with the others because his legs were weak, sat in a small chair on the hearth ; and when some extra piece of fun was up he would clap his little transparent hands, held on by nothing but " pipe-stems," as grandma said, and shrill out " Hurray ! " at the top of his feeble lungs.

The placid baby lay toasting on a quilt in front of the fire, with one ear growing as pink as a shell, while Linda went about touching the old familiar things softly with her hand. At last, when she came to the Squire's desk, with his well-worn leather-covered chair before it, and his plucky-looking old work-day hat and coat hanging above, she knelt down and hid her face in the cushions of the seat.

"Don't, Lindy," whispered the dame, bending over her. "Try to forget it to-day, deary."

"I can't, mother," was the broken reply. "He was always good to me before that happened, and I love him just the same."

"Yes, yes," was the answer; "he set great store by you, Lindy, for he said you had the spirit of the Northrups. There wasn't much mother in you," and the dame sighed and whisked away a tear.

Betsy Bingle, arrayed in her Sunday gown, with an astonishing yellow bow, which gave her the appearance of being pinned to a ticket, had as much as she could do to attend to what she called the boy's "shindys."

"Why don't you shut your fly-trap, Miss Bingle?" said Seth, the biggest boy—whom she considered head "skezecks"—as the openness of her countenance became more and more apparent.

"You're a sassy boy, and don't mind your manners," returned Betsy, with a snap; but, for all that, she laughed until the great brown turkey nearly slipped off the platter she was carrying.

O, I wonder if a dinner before or since ever looked, smelt, or tasted as gloriously as that dinner did to the sharp senses of Linda's little boys? It overflowed the big claw-footed dining-table, and went meandering away on sideboard and ancient half-round, in pies, and puddings, and shaking jellies.

"Hadn't I better keep on the watch, marm, for fear the old Squire should pop in?" whispered Betsy, coming to the back of the old lady's chair, where she sat with her eyes blurring at sight of the row of little expectant faces opposite, and Linda in her old place.

"Go along, Betsy Bingle, and take the baby," said the dame. "Don't be pestering, to spoil the comfort of this one day," she added in a lower tone. And after that I think they all forgot the existence of the Squire, even though his coat and stick seemed to menace them from the wall.

How I wish I could tell you of the way that dinner was eaten, of the fun and the frolic. How, when each of the little lads had a big plateful of turkey before him, a snicker ran along the line ; and, being reproved for it, how they declared it had snickered itself. How they stood themselves up, and shook themselves down, and began bravely all over again, until, when the great plum-cake was brought on, the weakly one got up on his shaky little pins, and cheered out sweet and shrill until the others all joined in, and grandma made a time of wiping her old eyes.

At last they were down on the hearth, cracking nuts and toasting apples, and Seth had pulled the old Squire's hat and coat off the hook to play wolf in, and was chasing Ben down a long side passage, when the breathless lad ran into a remarkably sturdy pair of old legs.

" Get along with your apple-cart," cried he, just as independent as a top wood-sawyer ; and the next moment something big and gruff collared him, and shook him smartly, and he looked up into a stern old face, fringed with white hair, surmounting a shaggy top-coat and muffler.

"Who be you, sauce-box?" growled a voice from the depths of the muffler.

"Ben Mason," said the boy promptly, looking up with his frank eyes, as if proud of the name.

The next moment he was whirled into a corner, and a terrible footstep went clumping down the passage.

"Massyful Peter! the old Squire has popped," screamed Betsy; and she let the baby fall just as the door burst in, revealing a white face quivering with passion. The blessed little thing set up an opportune squall, and the mother snatched it to her bosom and hid her face on its downy head, and the sturdy, manly little lads gathered about her, as if they meant to make a wall between mother and harm.

"So you came sneaking back, did you," cried the Squire, half-choked with rage, and at the same time pointing to her with his long, tremulous finger, "as soon as my face was turned? I didn't think you'd do it," he added, with bitter irony. "I had more respect for you."

"Don't blame her," cried the old wife, running and putting her hand on his arm. "I begged, and besought, and plead with her to come, because it has all been kept from the children, and I wanted them to feel there was a welcome for them in the old place on Thanksgiving day once before I died."

"You dared to do it!" he exclaimed, in a tone of unmitigated astonishment.

"Yes, Henry," and the old woman straightened up and met his eye without any break in her voice. "I was always afraid of you. You made me so the first day we were married ; but mother-love, they say, is as strong as death. It makes even such a poor creature as me brave. I couldn't have seen Lindy and her innocent children suffer if I'd died for helping them ; for aint they bone of my bone and flesh of my flesh ?" she cried, breaking into homely, touching pathos.

As the old woman gained in courage, with her face warming and glowing, the old man seemed to lose strength almost as if he had received a shock. The conflict of emotions, surprise, and bitter anger appeared to age him suddenly. He looked haggard and feeble, and groped about for a chair ; and then he sat down, and let his white head fall upon his hand.

"We must go away," sobbed Linda, as soon as she could speak. "After these long, hard years he hasn't a kind word to offer me, any more than if I was a stone."

The dazed children huddled closer together, and Seth put his arm around her waist. "Nobody shall touch my mother," said he, hotly; "let 'em try, if they darst to do it."

It was the clear Northrup ring; and the old Squire must have thought so, for he looked up.

"You can't let 'em go out into the cold and storm," (for it was snowing now in angry spits, and the sour day had grown sourer toward evening,) pleaded the dame. "You haven't the heart to see your own born child go out of the old door in bitter weather, with a baby in her arms and a sick boy ahold of her skirts. I know you too well, Henry Northrup. You can't hold such a grudge now that Ben is dead and buried; and on this day, when the Lord's mercies bid us forget and forgive."

The old man backed round away from the light.

" I 'spose she is ready now to say she's sorry for marrying that vagabones," he muttered, as if to the wall.

" No, never ! " cried Linda, starting up. " I should shame the old Northrup spirit if I did injustice to poor Ben, lying in his cold grave. There was bad luck all along, but he never spoke a cross word ; and when trouble came he took the half of every burden. Love helped us to bear it all."

She broke down worse than ever ; but by and by, as the Squire kept silence, with that bowed look upon him, she crept nearer to his chair, and somehow got into the circle of his arm, and laid her wet cheek and faded hair against his breast.

" Say you forgive me," she whispered. " I can go away and work for my little ones. I don't dread any thing that can happen ; only a father's wrath has weighed so heavy these many years."

The old man's head went lower and lower, and at last, when there was a sweet, solemn hush over the room, and Betsy Bingle was crying softly in the fireplace, he looked up with that altered face, that had aged and softened so in a single hour of deep experience, and said in that new way of referring to his wife, in a tone almost querulous and childish :

" Barbara, why don't you ask Lindy and the children to come and live with us here in the old place? Aint there room enough, I'd like to know? You have taken it all upon yourself, and you must fix things. You ought to have done it before, Barbara ; I should have been a better man. And now, is there time for God Almighty to have mercy on a hardened sinner ? "

" The Lord bless you, Henry," sobbed the old woman ; and then she got hold of his hand, and numbled it, and kissed it, and wet it all over with her happy tears. But presently the lumps cleared out of her throat, and she cried with almost girlish glee, " We have got the children home again in our old age, and it minds me to bless God for the sons and daughters that have gone back to old homes everywhere on this Thanksgiving Day."

" And may God remember those that are left in the cold away from mother's love and father's pity," murmured Linda.

" Hurray !" cheered the little weakly boy, not knowing exactly what he was cheering about; but it had the force of Amen. And there was the white-haired sire, with the worn daughter on his breast, and the blissful grand-dame, and the little rosy children, held in the sacred bond of our dear old Puritan festival, where the spirit of peace and love had turned the wrath of man to praise.

WIDOW HENDERSON'S HAPPENINGS.

———◆———

KNOCK, knock, knock, three times, and sharp too, upon the deal door which opened from the shady porch.

"I'm coming in just one minute." The voice that called out was pleasant and musical, and it made Aleck Gay's heart beat as no other could.

There was a little scramble within, and the noise of a whimpering child; then the door opened, and Mrs. Hetty Henderson stood holding the knob. She was snug and tidy, round and plump, though a little under size. Her hair was a rich auburn, of that smooth and tractable kind which never gets out of order. Her face was deliciously fair and rosy, or would have been but for a trace of weariness about the temples; and her eyes, of a warm hazel, would have brimmed over with smiles had not the white lids drooped a little from want of sleep. As she stood there, so unconsciously good and lovely, Aleck gave her a look of adoration.

"O, it's you, Aleck!" she said, simply.

"Yes, Hetty. I was going past on my way to Buxton, and I thought I'd let my horse bait long enough to inquire how you all are, and what has happened last; for you know, Hetty, something is always happening to you."

Mrs. Henderson let go the door and gave a laugh that sounded like the gurgle of a brook or the warble of a bobolink, or whatever is sweetest, only there was an under-tone of pathos in it, like a half sob, that went straight to Aleck's heart.

"Well, it beats all," said she. "I'm getting my name up; but something has happened, sure enough, this time. You know I was saying, just after that insurance company failed and refused to pay the money on poor Willie's life, the next thing to come along would be sickness. It was about time one of the children got down with something, and, sure enough, last Wednesday Ben was taken with the measles. He is as cross as two sticks, and I was up all last night giving him drink, and every hour I expect Hetty and Jane will come down, and my employer over in Buxton is hurrying me about those vests ; but I've been wonderfully helped through it all ; " and the blithe laugh came again, so gay and glad it almost brought the tears into Aleck's eyes.

"What a woman you are for looking on the bright side !" said he. "A body would think, to hear you talk, every time a trouble comes along that you had fallen heir to a first-class fortune."

"I should be pretty rich if that was so," responded Mrs. Henderson, "for something or other is always happening. I'm one of the sort the Bible speaks of—prone to trouble as the sparks are to fly upward. And yet I ought not to say that either, for I am wonderfully helped along."

"There's more practical religion in your little finger," said Aleck, admiringly, "than in the rest of the folks put together. But I guess I'll step in and take a chair, Hetty. It's as cheap sitting as standing any time."

The visitor walked into Mrs. Henderson's small sitting-room.

Overhead her little girls were playing at old

folks' tea-party, with broken dishes, and were having a very prim, formal, grown-up sort of time. The door was open into the bedroom, where the sick boy lay, and he now raised a half-disconsolate moan, for his mother to come and cool the hot pillow, and give him a drink of the slippery-elm tea which stood on the little stand by his side.

Aleck took off his hat, and wiped his forehead with a generous red silk handkerchief. He had a compact, well-shaped head, covered with crisp and curling-locks, a mottled, good-humored face, and when he smiled his mouth seemed full of white teeth. He was a little inclined to stoutness, and his neck-tie and waistcoat were not quite to Hetty's taste, and his trowsers showed rather too large and pronounced a plaid. Aleck was rather found of country balls and junketings. He liked a horse that held its head up and stepped out, and, on the other hand, he was not partial to long sermons. In the country neighborhood where he lived Aleck was considered a worldly man, clinging to the typical rags of self-righteousness. The parson made him a subject of prayer, and preached directly at him from the pulpit ; but still Aleck

believed in the good things of this life, and
never made professions of religion, much to the
sorrow of Hetty Henderson, who was a strict
Church-member, and, in spite of a conscience
morbidly tender, was filled with true, sweet
heart piety.

The little sitting-room was quite homely, but
some of the charm of Hetty's personality seemed
to cling about it, making it a veritable paradise
in Aleck's eyes. The windows were draped
with morning-glories and scarlet runners.
There was a chintz-covered lounge, and a
variety of splint-bottomed chairs with gay
patchwork cushions. In the pleasantest corner,
by the south window, where there came wafts
of the fragrance that is always floating about
in summer-time, and the speckled shade of
boughs and hum of bees and song of birds,
stood Hetty's sewing-machine. It was bright
and polished, and looked almost alive—as if it
could go alone. Aleck went over where it was
and sat down in the big rocking-chair, and laid
his hand on the case. He touched it with reverence, as if he would have liked to get down
on his knees and kiss the very treadle. There
was a kind of poetry about the mechanism in

his eye, for he knew all the brave, patient work it had performed, and the thought was too much for him.

"Confound it, Hetty!" he broke forth as Mrs. Henderson stepped from the bed-room, "I don't know how I'm going to stand it to have you work as you do. You understand how it has been with me ever since we were children together. I wouldn't speak until a year after poor Will's death."

Hetty turned and gave him a pleading look.

"Forgive me," said he, penitent to the very toes of his big boots. "I'm an awkward, clumsy fellow, Hetty, and it's just like me to tread on a flower when I would give my right hand to save it. But you know how I have always felt since we went to school together and ate out of the same luncheon-basket, and I gathered nuts and wild cherries for you in summer, and dragged you up hill on my sled in winter. There came a time, Hetty, when you told me you could not love me, and I never blamed you for taking Will. He was worthier, far worthier, than I. I tried hard not to envy him, even when it was the worst with me, and I don't say but what I did enjoy life some. I'm no hypocrite,

11

Hetty," he went on, humbly, "and a wrong word will slip out now and then when I am angry. I am sorry for it, Hetty. I wish I was a better man, and I know you could make me one. I don't make professions, and I never have signed a temperance pledge, because I think a man's character is pledge enough against his making a beast of himself. The pharisees call me hard names, for a man's reputation is blasted in this community if he uses a check-rein and occasionally takes a glass of hard cider. If I don't make any pretense to piety, I'm straighter in my business dealings than some round here that do."

Hetty did not like this kind of talk, and her face showed it. The softness departed, and a look of decision and character came in its stead.

"Your can't clear your own skirts," said she, with a little asperity, " by throwning blame on professors of religion. If you do see a mote in your neighbor's eye, that isn't going to pluck the beam out of your own eye."

Aleck saw he had upset his own dish, and inwardly groaned. " I didn't mean that, Hetty," he broke out. "I know I'm a miserable sinner.

There was a time when I thought I should be lost. It was after poor Will was shot in the battle of the Wilderness, and you were left to struggle on alone, and I saw your white face before me, and I was almost crazy. But after a year or two it seemed to me I might begin to hope. I thought how I could take you and the children home, and keep trouble and want away, and just live and breathe to make you happy, until I felt sure you could save me from selfishness and make me a new creature."

Aleck saw a little flicker in Hetty's face, and it induced him to go on in a more impassioned strain of pleading.

" I sometimes have thought, Hetty," said he, " that my love for you is kind of religious. I can't see God, but I can see his goodness shining in your eyes. There's many a man around her who expects to get to heaven on the strength of his wife's prayers. If I was hard pushed to say what there is in me that deserves heaven, I should have to confess there's nothing but my constant love for the best woman in the world. If my heart was laid open to your pure eyes, you would see how all that is good and honest in me goes out toward you, O,

some folks can steer right along toward heaven
of themselves ; they are strong and full of
faith.   Other folks must have something to
catch hold of—it may be a little child's hand,
or a woman's heart, but it is a very real thing ;
and I tell you what it is, Hetty, I do believe you
could tow me right along into glory."

Aleck was not quite a gentleman, not very
refined ; but the yearning, the passion, the faith
of the man wrought upon his face and made it
noble.   Hetty would have been less than woman
had she remained unmoved.

"You do wrong, Aleck," said she, gently,
"to put a poor, erring, weak creature in the
place of the Creator.   Be careful that you do
not grieve away the Spirit of God.   Your heart
is set on the things of this world, I fear, and it
is your duty to wait more faithfully on the
means of grace."

"I will do any thing on earth you want me
to, Hetty," Aleck responded with alacrity.   "I'll
go to meeting every Sunday if you'll let me sit
beside you and look over the same hymn-book.
Ding it all, I'll turn missionary to the canni-
bals, if you will, and go off to Injy, or any other
place where they eat human beefsteaks.   I

could go to jail with you, Hetty, and think myself a happy man."

"You make light of serious things," said
Hetty, very gravely, taking up the hem of her
apron and putting it together in little folds.
Then she happened to glance out of the window at the yellow-wheeled sulky, which was
abominable in her eyes. Aleck's sorrel horse
was backing in the thills, impatient for the appearance of his master. "We don't think alike,
Aleck," she continued, looking down at a red
stripe in the carpet, "and I fear we shall
never agree on the most important things. I
know how large and generous your heart is,
and prize its worth ; but I cannot feel it is right
for us to marry. The Bible says, 'Be ye not
unequally yoked with unbelievers.' I shall pray
for your conversion, as I have been doing for a
long time."

Hetty's voice faltered, and Aleck got up and
broke abruptly into the middle of her sentence.
"Don't think I'm going to take this for your
final answer, Hetty. There's hope as long as
there's life. I do believe you love me a little,
way down deep in your heart ; and if I was a
miserable wretch just fit for the hospital or poor-

house, you would think it your duty to marry me, and take up your cross and earn my support, for your soul's good.   But here I am, a great, strong man with enough and to spare, ready to lift you out of a life of drudgery, and give you every comfort, and educate the children, and love you with my whole heart and soul and strength, and you will persist in turning me off because you are afraid of offending the Lord. I don't believe the Lord is offended by such things, and you ought to follow the dictates of your heart."

He strode to the door, and slammed it as he went out; and Hetty, whose nerves were a little shaky from watching the previous night, sat down in the rocking-chair and buried her burning face in her hands.   Aleck had treated her outrageously.   He was positively brutal.   How dared he say he believed she loved him a little down deep in her heart?   The thought of the insult she had received made the tears flow and trickle through her fingers.   Aleck had widened the breach between them, and as she was sure she didn't love him, there was no apparent need of grieving over it.   She knew she should be wonderfully helped, for she always was, and yet somehow she felt very low-spirited and miserable. There was a great pile of vests to stitch for her employer at Buxton, and the work must be done in time, even though her head did ache and her eyes blur with weariness.

Aleck, for his part, threw himself into the yellow sulky, and gave the sorrel horse his head. As he turned away from the little red farm-house, where such a patient, sweet life was being lived, he felt heartily ashamed of himself because he was so prosperous·and well off, with a great stock-farm clear from debt, the best stone house in the township, and money in bank. He was disgusted with his stout limbs and excellent digestion. If he had been born halt or blind, Hetty might have taken him home to her heart. She had married Will Henderson, he felt sure, because he was the best and unluckiest fellow in the world.

The hay harvest was over, and the fields were smoothly shorn. Elms by the wayside seemed to drip with golden light. The cardinal-flower looked at its splendid image in the lazy little brook that flowed along coquetting with alders and reeds. There were good farms on either side the way. Aleck crossed the covered bridge

over a wide, shallow stream, and came out on a
bit of smooth road and an old brown barn with
doors wide open abutting almost upon the track.
Two or three farmers had gathered to inspect a
horse which the owner of the place—a tall,
black-whiskered man—in his shirt sleeves, had
brought out from the stable. A passer-by in a
light democrat wagon slued his vehicle round
out of the road, and stopped to observe what was
going on. Aleck did the same with his yellow-
wheeled sulky, for his instinct scented a trade.
The animal on exhibition was a tall chestnut,
clean-limbed, with a shiny satin coat, and a peculiarly wicked eye.

"What will you take for that horse, Bates?"
inquired Aleck, after he had exchanged nods
with the neighbors.

"Wa'al, I don't know just what I would
take. I vally him purty high. He's a nice
horse, but he aint just the beast to work on a
farm. Now if you want to swap off that there
sorrel of yours, I wouldn't mind giving a little
boot."

"Come, now, out with it, Bates; let's know
what ails him! Is he spavined, or broken-
winded?"

" No," said one of the old farmers, whose face looked like a carved walnut, at the same time ejecting a liberal shower of tobacco juice, " he's as sound as a nut, not five years old, but you see he's got a leetle touch of the devil in him. Mebbe for a week he'll go along as steady as an old cow, and then he'll take a notion to, kick and stiffen his hind legs like steel crow-bars, and, you'd better believe, any thing that's be-hind him is pretty likely to be sent to kingdom come. When he takes it into his head to run, a chain of lightnin' wouldn't hold him ; and every now and then he breaks his headstall all to flinders, and chaws up his grain-bin."

"You needn't make it out worse than it is," said Bates in a grieved tone. " I don't kalker-late to deceive any body about this here animal. I never said he was a likely animal, and I aint a-going to have a neighbor, after he's got his neck broke, and been sot on by a crowner and twelve men, come and prosecute me for damages; but if he's willing to trade, knowing all the facts, why, that's his own look-out."

" How much boot will you give ? " inquired Aleck, laconically.

"Why, for that there sorrel of yours," said

Mr. Bates, " I wouldn't mind a cool hundred and fifty down, or, what's the same thing, a check for that amount on Buxton Bank."

"Agreed!" returned Aleck, and he threw down the lines and sprang out of the sulky. " Here, untackle my horse and put in yours, and then we will go over to the house and square up the money matters."

Two weeks slipped away, and the Widow Henderson saw nothing of Aleck Gay. Things had happened all along—not the brightest and happiest things, but smiles still shone in Hetty's eyes, though more and more tremulous with tears. The two little girls had fallen sick of measles, and the disease seemed to go very hard with Jenny, the youngest, the baby and pet. Anxiety and constant watching had worn upon Hetty's nerves, and some of the work for her Buxton employer was done when she was ready to drop to sleep over the machine. One parcel of vests had already found their way back, with a sharp note, saying the stitching did not give satisfaction, and must be done over ; and, worse than all, the post had brought her an official document from Washington, with the information that, on account of some irregularity in his papers, poor

Will's pension, which had been continued to his widow, was about to be withdrawn. It might cost more time and money than she had to spare to get the claim re-established. The old farmhouse where she lived had only a few rather productive acres attached to it, and was beavily mortgaged. Hetty had depended upon the pension to keep down the interest, and now there was a bleak, homeless prospect staring her and her little brood in the face. But all the time she knew she should be wonderfully helped through her troubles. The thought of Aleck Gay—great, generous-hearted fellow—who had loved her so faithfully long years, came like a warm, sweet suffusion, and burnt upon her cheek in a hidden blush. Hetty suspected this feeling was a temptation in disguise, for she knew the devil has a very ungentlemanly way of taking advantage of a woman's weak back and tired feet.

Near Hetty's house was an ugly, steep hill, with more pitches and shelving banks than any other in half a day's journey. That same afternoon, which was lowering and overcast, an old man in a tow frock was guiding a pair of oxen down Long Hill. When about half-way to the bottom his bleary old eyes took note of some-thing ahead which looked like the detached wheels and body of a yellow sulky. His slow senses had scarcely made this observation when he came upon a man, hatless, and with torn coat, lying among some loose stones a little under the bank.

"Why, du tell, if it aint Aleck Gay!"

"It's me, sure enough," groaned Aleck. "That beast of mine ran away and smashed the sulky to shivers. I hope he has broken his confounded neck. My ankle is sprained, and I have hurt my arm, and there are some scratches on my face, but I hope my bones are all right.   Come, daddy, give me a lift as far as the Widow Henderson's, and on your way home you may stop at the doctor's."

Hetty had just put down little Jane, after a bad coughing fit, when there came a confused and ominous sound from the front porch. She ran to the door, and, throwing it open, called out, in a tone of despair, "What has happened now?"

"It's me, Hetty," Aleck answered as he was being helped in. "I met with an accident near here, and am pretty well knocked to pieces, and

I thought, seeing how it is, you would not refuse to take me in."

Hetty reeled back against the side of the passage-way without speaking, and turned very pale. Aleck saw the look, and it made his heart leap up in his throat, although he was suffering considerable pain. Soon the patient was sitting bolstered up in a rocking-chair, wrapped in a blanket, with his hurt foot on a cushion and pillows about him. Arnica, camphor, lint, and bandages were quickly brought; Hetty washed the blood from his forehead with a very tender touch.

"Aleck," inquired she sympathetically, "don't you think it would do you good to have a plaster on these cuts?"

"No," said Aleck, giving a prodigious groan, "it aint worth while. Only if you would stand there and hold your hand on my head a few minutes, it would draw better than any plaster in the world."

"You need some thing warming to take inwardly, Aleck. I am afraid you will get exhausted and faint away."

" No"—and he gave another profound sigh— " but if you'll sit down there, where I can look at you handy, it will do me more good than doctor's stuff."

Hetty sat down accordingly, and as the pity grew in her face, hope rose in the breast of Aleck.

"Do you think your leg is broken, Aleck? I am so sorry for your sufferings. The pain must be intense."

"It is pretty bad," answered Aleck, evasively, "and I can't tell just what has happened until the doctor comes. I've a notion it's mostly internal. There is something wrong here," and he put his hand conspicuously over his heart. "I don't know but I'm going to pieces. One thing is certain; I never shall ride in that yellow sulky again. It may be all day. with me;" and then came another dreadful groan. "Hetty"—after a little pause—"don't you think you could reconcile it with your sense of duty to take pity on me? You accept misfortunes so beautifully, Hetty; now I have become—a—a kind of misfortune, couldn't you accept me?"

"If I can do you good," said Hetty timidly. "It would seem almost providential. Who knows but this may prove a means of grace?"

"It will!" cried Aleck in ecstasy. He quite forgot to groan, and with his sound arm he clasped her waist. "Hetty, God helping me, this shall prove the best thing that ever happened to you."

HANNAH'S QUILTING.

———◆———

HANNAH thought she knew the state of Fred Freeman's heart. She had trifled with him a little, and her own mind was not quite made up.

She was sitting now in her chamber, sweet and clean with whitewash and new buff paper, and bowery with green light which fell from the pear-tree boughs through freshly-starched muslin curtains. Hannah was a nice-looking blonde maiden, dressed in a tidy chocolate print, with a blue bow nestling in her thick, wavy hair. She had been writing a note by the stand, and was sealing it with one of the motto seals then in fashion. This one said, " Come ;" and it was easy to see that it indorsed a note of invitation.

She ran down stairs into the fresh morning air, where her father, Deacon Ashley, was just ready to head old Charley toward the village.

Her mother, a buxom matron, was standing bare-headed beside the democrat wagon, hand- ing up the molasses jug, and charging the Deacon not to forget that pound of Castile soap and the lamp-wicks. Hannah tucked up her trim skirts, and ran out through the dewy grass.

"See here, father," she called, in her pleasant voice, "you must stop at the school-house and give this note to Andy Freeman. It's for Jane, you know, asking her and Miss Lang to come to the quilting."

"Aint there one for Fred Freeman, too?" inquired the good-natured old Deacon, with a wink.

"I told Jane he could come in the evening if he chose," returned Hannah, with slightly heightened color. "Doctor Bingham will be here," she added, "and some other young men."

"Fred Freeman is worth the whole kit," re- sponded the Deacon; "and that young pill-box, according to my way of thinking, runs too much to hair-ile and watch-chains; but Fred has got good hard sense and first-rate learning. He can appear with any of 'em. If you don't look

12

out, Han, he'll be shining round that pretty
girl from Hillsdale."

"It makes no difference to me who he
shines round," returned Hannah, with a slight
shade of offense; but, nevertheless, there was
a little pang at her heart as she turned back
toward the house. Hannah's mind was not quite
easy about Jane Freeman's visitor, the pretty
girl from Hillsdale, but she thought if she
could see Fred and Mary Lang together, she
would know in just what quarter the wind was
setting.

The Deacon tucked the note into his breast-
pocket, took the molasses jug between his feet,
and gave old Charley a cut with the lines pre-
paratory to making him begin to move, an operation of some length, as Charley believed the
Deacon to be under his orders. At last, however, the two were trotting and rattling past the
goose-pond, and the big barns, and the tall elms
that cast some very cool shadows across the
brown dust of the road, until, with a kind of
mutual understanding and sympathy, they came
out against a stretch of post and rider fence,
inclosing a field of the biggest kind of clover.

It looked like good farming to the Deacon's

eyes. He could calculate pretty closely the number of tons of sweet, juicy feed there would be to the acre ; and yet this morning the fragrance, and the rosy bloom and the hum of insects among the thick heads, brought him a different kind of pleasure.

With the long sight of age he could see the cows grazing in the back pasture, and he thought of the " cattle on a thousand hills," and whose they are. His gaze wandered back lovingly even to the old stone walls with mulleins growing beside them, and the shadows of birds flitting over them, and every thing seemed good, even the May-weed, and daisies, and Canada thistles that farmers hate by instinct. He felt a gush of childlike thankfulness, because " the earth is the Lord's, and the fullness thereof."

Presently the Deacon and Charley came across a group of school-children — brown, freckle-faced little urchins, in calico shirts, tow trowsers, and shilling hats much the worse for wear. Then there was a tall red-headed girl who had out-grown all the tucks in her dress, and had torn her apron in following the boys over the wall after a chipmunk ; and one or two little tots, with very flappy sun-bonnets, whose short legs would not allow them to keep up. They all carried dinner-pails and dog's-eared spelling-books, and at the very end of the string there was a low-spirited yellow dog.

" Whoa!" cried the Deacon, setting his two boots-soles, which resembled weather-beaten scows, against the dash-board, and pulling in hard—an operation Charley did not at all relish, although he at last yielded, with a shake of his homely head, which intimated it was done by special favor, and could not be repeated.

" Jump in, children!" cried the good-natured old man ; " I'll give ye a lift as far as the school-house. Beats all how much little shavers think of ketchin' a ride. There, don't crowd, boys. Let the girls in first, and mind your manners ; " and he lifted in a little roly-poly maid, with pin-cushion hands and a very suggestive stain of wild cherries around her dimpled mouth, and seated her on the buffalo beside him. The others all tumbled in in a trice.

" 'Pears to me I wouldn't eat them puckery things," said the Deacon in his grandfatherly fashion, pointing to some suggestive smears on the little maid's high gingham apron. " They'll give you the colic."

" Yes, sir," answered the child, folding her funny little hands contentedly in her lap. " Sissy had the measles and I didn't, and my mother said I might have the colic if I wanted to."

The Deacon leaned back and laughed, and Charley shook his ears and turned up at him an eye of mild reproach.

" What a little goose you are ! " said a bright-faced boy, who had been very much squeezed in the legs, and had just administered several sharp punches in the side of the squeezer as he leaned over the back of the seat to pinch the little girl's ear.

" Bless me ! there's Andy Freeman, and I had like to have forgot the what-d'ye-call-it— billy-do—my Hannah sent to the girls up at your house."

The Deacon veered half round and checked Charley, who by this time began to consider the whole thing disgusting, especially as the low-spirited dog had mixed himself up with his feet.

" This must be it," he went on, fumbling in

his pocket. "You see I've left my best eyes at home; the old pair I carry in my head don't amount to much."

Andy took the folded paper, and promised to be careful of it; and by the time Charley and his load had arrived at the stone school-house, which looked very much like a juvenile penitentiary, the schoolmistress was standing in the door ringing the bell; and the children scrambled down the side of the wagon and scampered off, to save their marks for punctuality.

Jane Freeman had been busy all day with her friend Mary Lang, the pretty girl from Hillsdale. There is nothing at first so engrossing to the mind of a country girl as the stylish clothes of her city visitor. Mary had a number of fashionably-made dresses, and, as old Mrs. Freeman remarked, she had got the "very latest quirk" in her pretty hair. She was a good-natured girl, and had let Jane cut the pattern of her visite and her tabbed muslin cape, and had shown her just how to do the captivating twist. Now the two girls were bending out of the sitting-room window, which looked upon the orchard, with its gnarled boughs, and cool green lights, and white clover-heads dropped

upon the grass like unstrung pearls. Fred had
come up from the garden, and was leaning on
his hoe-handle, talking to them. He was a
muscular, well-made young fellow; and the fact
that he had once passed three years in a city,
and had rubbed off his rustic bashfulness, told
upon him well. Now there was a half-quizzical,
half-pleased look peeping out from under
his drooped eyelids; and old Mrs. Freeman,
sitting on the back porch, with her glasses in
the fold of a magazine story, and the toe of one
of her husband's socks covering her knobby fin-
ger-ends, glanced at the group, and thought to
herself that Mary Lang, with all her finery,
wouldn't be sorry to catch Fred. Then at the
memory of Hannah Ashley there came a little
twinge of anxiety; for Hannah was her prime
favorite; and, after the manner of substantial
matrons, she desired her boy to marry a practical wife, who knew how to cook his dinner and
make him comfortable. The sight of Mary
Lang's white nerveless hands, with their pretty
rings, caused the old lady to shake her head,
and mutter something about " dolls and pop-
pets."

Andy had come home from school, and had

let the low-spirited dog out into the back lot to bark at the hens a little while by way of wholesome recreation. He was preparing to go down to his squirrel-trap in the woods; and as he sat fussing away and whistling on the porch step, suddenly he pulled a paper out of his jacket pocket, and scampered off with it to the window.

"Here's something Deacon Ashley told me to give you, Sis. He called it a billy."

"You mean a William," put in Mary, chucking him under the chin.

"Why it's nothing but that advertisement of Puffer's Pills the Deacon promised father! I thought Hannah would be sure to invite us to her quilting," said Jane in a disappointed tone "Say, Fred, have you and Han been quarreling?" and she gave him a provoking little thrust, such as sisters are wont to administer.

Fred turned round and set his elbows squarely against the window-sill, and began to whistle low to himself.

"Let's take that ride over to Saddleback Hill I promised to give you to-morrow afternoon, Mary," said he, veering back again and chewing a stalk of grass."

Miss Lang expressed herself delighted to take the ride ; and every body appeared satisfied but Jane, who now would have no opportunity to display the new twist to the girls before Sunday.

Hannah's quilt had been put on the frames the day before, up in the spare chamber—a large apartment with a carpet in Venetian stripe, a high-post bedstead draped in the whitest dimity, a heavy mahogany bureau with respectable brass knobs, and an old-fashioned glass adorned with festoons of pink and white paper. There were faded foot-stools, worked by Mrs. Ashley, when a girl, in chain-stitch embroidery ; and framed samplers and silhouette portraits upon the wall of a cappy old lady and a spare old gentleman ; and matronly bunches of life-everlasting and crystallized grasses filling the plethoric vases upon the mantel-piece. Every thing was in apple-pie order from kitchen to parlor. A pleasant, moist odor of Hannah's sponge-cake clung to the walls ; and if you don't know what Hannah's sponge-cake was like, it is useless for me to describe it.

Hannah had put on her prettiest lawn dress —a pale green that became her blonde beauty, and touched it up here and there with a bit of pink ribbon. Mrs. Ashley was pinning on her false puffs before the glass, and fastening her collar with a brooch adorned with a daguerreo-type likeness of the Deacon, which looked as if it had been taken in a particularly bad fit of dyspepsia. She dearly loved young company ; and there was a bright twinkle in her eye, and a pucker about her mouth, provocative of jokes.

When the girls had assembled, and the kiss-ing and taking off of things was well through with, the grand business of the afternoon began. Every body praised Hannah's pretty quilt— pink stars dropped on to a white ground. Miss Treadwell was champion quilter. She under-stood all the mysteries of herrin'-bone and feather patterns ; and, with a chalk-line in her hand, as the Deacon's wife expressed it, " ruled the roost." Miss Treadwell was a thin-faced-precise old maid, with a kind of withered bloom on her cheek-bones, and a laudable desire to make the most of her few skimpy locks.

" Beats all how young Salina Treadwell appears," whispered the Deacon's wife to her next neighbor. " She's as old as I be if she's

9601 Hannah's Quilting Party.

When the kissing was well through with, the grand business of the
afternoon began.

a day, and here she goes diddling round with the girls."

"Hannah, you ought to give this quilt to the one that gets married first," put in Susan Drake, threading her needle.

"I know who that will be," said Mrs. Ashley, winking hard toward Hetty Sprague, a pretty, soft-headed little maiden, with cheeks of the damask-rose and dewy, dark eyes.

"O, Miss Ashley!" cried Hetty, simpering sweetly, "how can you talk so? You know I never mean to get married all my born days. Men are such deceitful creatures!"

Miss Treadwell heaved a deep sigh, and snapped the chalk-line sentimentally, as if she too could a tale unfold that would tell of the perfidy of the male sex.

"I don't, for my part, see why every thing should be given to the married folks," returned Hannah, tapping lightly on the frame with her thimble, and feeling annoyed because Jane Freeman and her friend had not yet put in an appearance. "When I get to be an old maid I'll stuff every thing soft with feathers and wool, and keep sixteen cats, like Aunt Biceps."

"You an old maid!" cried merry little Nancy Duffy. "That's a likely story. I guess Fred will have a word or two to say about it."

"It looks as if Fred had got a new string to his bow," remarked Miss Treadwell, who knew how to give a sharp little thrust of her own. "He appears to be mighty thick with that girl from Hillsdale."

"Why, there goes Fred now!" cried Hetty Sprague; and the girls ran to the window, upsetting one end of the quilt, just in time to see Fred's sleek chestnut mare trot past, with Fred himself so absorbed in the companion by his side that he did not appear to remark the battery of bright eyes under which he was passing.

Hannah colored and bit her lips, but she recovered herself with a light laugh.

"Never mind, girls," said she; "there are as good fish in the sea as ever have been caught. I'll show you Doctor Bingham to-night, and you'll all say he is perfectly splendid."

Then began a little mild gossip over the Doctor, as to who he was, and what had brought him to out-of-the-way Drastic—for the young man was only a visitor in the neighborhood—

and in the clatter of tongues, before the second rolling, Hannah had slipped out to get tea. At first she did a very curious thing for a sensible young woman to do. She got behind the buttery-door and hid her face in the roller-towel, and something very like a genuine sob shook her bosom, while some bitter tears were absorbed into the crash. The truth is, Hannah was jealous. The sight of Fred devoting himself to that girl from Hillsdale, whom she had begun to detest, woke her up to the state of her own feelings, and perhaps nothing but that would ever have done the work.

Nevertheless, there was the sponge-cake to cut, and the best doyleys to be got out, and the ivory-handled knives to be taken down from the top shelf of the closet. She had to caleulate how much of the strawberry preserves it would take to go round and not look skimpy, and who should sit by the glass dish, and how many custard cups would be required to fill the middle of the table. All these things Hannah performed with as much accuracy as if her heart had not been smarting with disappointment and vexation.

Mrs. Ashley was never more in her element

than when she presided at a feminine tea-party.

"We wont have any of the men folks round to bother, girls," said she as they settled like a flock of doves about the table, which Hannah had so temptingly spread. "It's busy times on the farm now, and the Deacon likes a · bite of something hearty for his tea, so I told him he and the boys might wait. Ahem, Salina, do you take sugar in your tea?" as she poured out a cup of the delicate green flavored beverage that diffused an appetizing fragrance through the room.

"O, Miss Ashley," cried Nancy Duffy, "you'll tell our fortunes, wont you? There isn't a soul here to know about it, and we'll keep as whist as mice."

"Now, girls, don't make me appear simple," said Mrs. Ashley, leaning back and wiping her red and smiling face free from the steam of the tea-pot. "If Miss Whitcomb should get hold of it she'd say it didn't become a deacon's wife."

"Never mind Miss Whitcomb," broke in Susan Drake. "She thinks she's arrived at perfection, and such folks are always disagreeable. Here, do look at Salina Treadwell's cup. If I'm not mistaken there's an offer in it."

"Of course there is," said Mrs. Ashley, taking up the cup with professional interest. "Don't you see that ring, almost closed, with a heart inside? And she's going to accept it. It's coming from a light-complected man. Looks a little like Sile Winthrop, down at the the Corners."

"O, Miss Ashley, how you do talk!" cried Salina, mincing her biscuit and blushing up on her cheek-bones.

"He aint a-going to live long, whoever it is," the Deacon's wife went on, twirling the cup with the girls hanging over her shoulder, and her eyes dancing with fun. "Yes, Salina, you will be left a widder."

"What a sad thing it must be to lose a companion," put in sentimental Ann Davis. "I should hate to be left a relic."

"Never you mind, Salina," the Deacon's wife continued, with a wink. "If I'm not mistaken you'll console yourself with number two. Look there, girls, at the true-lovers' knot and the bow and arrers."

Miss Treadwell held up her hands in mock horror, and affirmed that she didn't believe a word of it; but it was noticeable, as Mrs. Ashley said, that she was "chipperer" all the rest of the evening.

"Come, now tell Hannah's," cried Hetty Sprague. So Hannah passed along her cup.

"Why, child, you're going to shed tears, and there's a little cloud of trouble round you; but it will clear away, and you'll get your wish in spite of every thing."

"Don't you see saddle-bags and pill-boxes there?" inquired Nancy Duffy.

"Go along with your stuff and nonsense, girls!" exclaimed the Deacon's wife, waving away the cup. "If husband should get hold of it he'd say I was trifling."

That evening, after Doctor Bingham had fooled a good deal with Hannah—had pressed her hand at parting, and whispered he should hope to see her next evening at the singing-class —she remembered her fortune, and did let some bitter tears soak into her pillow. She was not wise enough in worldly ways to suspect that the Doctor, a town-bred man, had set Hetty Sprague's silly little heart a-fluttering while he

walked home with her under the warm starlight, although, in very truth, he did not care a
fip for either of them.   Hannah was content to
play him off against Fred, let the consequences
be what they might; and more and more as she
thought the matter over, she blamed that design-
ing girl from Hillsdale.

The next night set in with a mild drizzle;
and, in spite of Mrs. Ashley's protestations,
Hannah was off to the singing-class.   This
class had been established to improve the church
music, which, as the Deacon said, sadly needed
" tinkering; " and gradually it became a resort
for the young people of the village, while its
functions were stretched to include a good deal
of mild flirtation.   Hannah, on entering, looked
anxiously round to discover the Doctor; but,
strange to say, he was absent.   Fred, who belonged to the choir, sat in his usual place alone.
Neither Jane nor her young lady visitor had
accompanied him.   These facts Hannah ascer-
tained before she let her eyes drop on her note-
book.   She watched the door keenly all through
the hour of practice; but the Doctor did not
make his appearance, and her indignation grew
apace.   She hoped to slip away, a little in ad-

vance of the crowd, before the exercises were quite over, and the cordon of young men had formed about the entrance. But just as she was stepping off into the darkness, with the warm rain falling steadily, a hand touched her arm.

"Let me walk home with you, Hannah. I have an umbrella, and you are unprovided." It was Fred's voice; and Hannah was nettled to remark not even a touch of penitence in its tone.

"No, I thank you," she returned, stiffly. "I prefer to go alone."

"But you cannot refuse my company for a few steps, at least," said he, pushing up his umbrella and shielding her whether or no, "for I have brought an apology from Bingham. I am going to tell you, as a great secret," Fred went on, confidentially, while Hannah kept still from sheer astonishment, "that the Doctor and that forty-'leventh cousin of ours, from Hillsdale, were engaged once. The Doctor's a capital fellow, but there's a jealous streak in him. He wanted to keep a loose foot, and wasn't willing Mary should do the same. She's an uncommonly pretty, lively girl"—a sharp twinge in Hannah's left side—"and, of course, she wasn't going to be cooped up, and the result was they quarreled. But they did really care for each other, and now the thing is made up, and I guess they have found out what a sneaking, unrighteous thing jealousy is."

"There might be cause for it," returned Hannah, faintly, as she felt her spirit oozing away.

"Come now, Hannah, you mean to hit me, and I might hit back again, but I wont, for I haven't loved any body but you—just as much as you would let me—ever since I was a boy. I am one of the constant kind. Don't you know I am, Hannah?"—very softly spoken for such a big fellow. "My heart has learned one trick of loving, and it can't unlearn it."

"Why, sir, didn't you and Jane come to my quilting party?"—spoken in a shaky voice, and showing the white feather badly—"and why did you go gallivanting off with that girl?"

"You did not ask us, in the first place, and that girl was a visitor, and I liked her."

"Don't be saucy. I sent a note to Jane, and told father to give it to Andy."

"Ha, ha!" laughed Fred, "it is all explained now. The old gentleman sent us an advertisement of Puffer's Pills by mistake, and you will find the note quietly reposing in his pocket."

I am afraid Fred was saucy, for when Hannah got into the house there was something very sweet and delicious tingling upon her lips. She crept into the sitting-room, where she could hear the good old Deacon calmly snoring, and slipped the little note out of the breast pocket of his coat.

Long afterward, when she had been Fred's wife many a year, and the colors of the pretty star-quilt had faded upon her bed, Hannah would take the little billet, grown yellow now, from an inner drawer, where she kept it along with a silky tress cut from the head of the baby she had lost, and kiss it tenderly, as if new faith and trust could emanate from its folds.

THE GOOD-BYE KISS.

THE through night-train on the "Great Northern" was within ten minutes of starting time.

The steam-whistle had given its first premonitory shriek, passengers were hurrying in with bags and shawls, and the demand for seats was becoming lively.

Among those who entered the sleeping-car just at this moment was a young man, and a girl—evidently his sister—some two or three years younger than himself.

They were neither of them handsome, or in any way noticeable, except as possessing earnest faces, marked with intelligence and the lines of early care.

"Here is your berth, Milly. I secured a whole one, because I knew you would not like being put with a stranger. And I bought you a picture paper and some oranges to beguile the way."

"Thank you, Ralph. You are very thoughtful of my little comforts. I do not dread this journey a bit; and you know, generally, I am rather timid about traveling."

Ralph was busy arranging Milly's things on the opposite seat. "Of course you'll write immediately, and let me know how you get through to Fulham, and how you find things."

"O, certainly; be assured of that. I shall have Saturday and Sunday to look about, and get acquainted, before I begin my school Monday morning. You shall have a faithful report of all I see and hear."

"Well"—and the young man stood with his hand on the back of the seat, looking rather nervously at the door, as if afraid of being carried off—"take care of yourself, and keep up good courage."

"Never fear about that, Ralph; and I beg of you to take care of yourself and not overwork." Milly's voice trembled the least bit, in spite of her show of bravery.

"O, don't fret on my account," returned the brother. "A man can always get along." This was said with a touch of superiority, as if his male condition ought to put him beyond the reach of a woman's solicitude.

The girl's eyes grew a little misty and wistful. Perhaps Ralph did not see it. " There!" said he, as a long shiver ran through the train, " I must be off. Good-bye!"

"Good-bye!" They shook hands; the car door banged; Ralph was gone.

" O dear!" sighed Milly, and she hastily got up and went over to the opposite window. The train was jerking now like a victim of St. Vitus' dance. There Ralph stood among hackmen, porters, and baggage trucks. How preoccupied and tired he looked! Milly sighed more deeply than ever as she tried in vain to catch his eye. There comes a long defiant shriek from the engine, with a crescendo which says " Positively the last." They are moving off. He sees her now and waves his hand, his face lit up with something like real interest and affection.

Now the train crawls, like a long, many-jointed worm, out of the smoky depot. Milly has lost sight of her brother, so she sinks back into her own particular corner, and begins to feel very miserable and desolate.

" I wish Ralph had kissed me good-bye." That was the thought uppermost in Milly's mind, and it brought a few very real, positive tears to her

eyes.   The sleeping-car was but comfortably
filled, and this circumstance, with the arrangement of the berths, secured to the young traveler a very grateful sense of privacy.   Life was
all before her—all to win.   A few weeks before,
the position in the Fulham high-school she had
since secured had seemed the one thing needful
to her happiness.   Now it had lost a little of its
rose hue, and the dreary struggle for self-sup-
port, which orphanage and poverty forced upon
her, stretched out a bleak perspective.   She began to realize that it meant separation from her
brother, the only near relative now remaining
to her on earth.   Their life-ways had begun di-
verging, and who could say if they would ever
again become one, as in years gone by ?

Some very old sources of pain, some very
secret pangs, awoke in Milly's mind as she sat
with her head resting against the window, and
a thick blue vail drawn over her face.   They all
resolved themselves into that but half-acknowl-
edged regret—" I am so sorry Ralph didn't kiss
me good-bye ! "

There was much mutual respect and esteem
between this brother and sister, but not that
frank and free intimacy which perhaps more

frequently exists between those unallied by blood than between the members of one household. Milly always felt conscious of the fact that she did not quite come up to Ralph's standard of young ladyhood, and it made her plainer and quieter to him than to other people. He knew she was the best girl in the world, with five times as much sense in her head as all the gay butterflies of his native town put together; but his eyes informed him that she was neither pretty nor exactly graceful, and that she did not possess the art of dressing with elegance on a very insufficient sum of pocket-money.

Ralph possessed a keen love of beauty, and an intense desire to rise in the world. He knew that some day he should push his way to fortune; and his sister, he felt, ought to be able to grace any position in life. It chafed him bitterly that he could not at once furnish her an ample support, which would take away the necessity for daily drudging in the school-room.

Often, when he came home at night dissatisfied, moody, and silent, there, in the shabby little sitting-room, sat Milly, with her tired, patient face bent over her work, perhaps a new shirt for himself or some garment for her own wearing, which ten busy fingers made haste to construct in the few hours allotted for such tasks.

A tired man likes to be amused, and too often forgets that a tired woman has the same need of diversion as himself. If Milly had been more positively cheerful and light-hearted, perhaps Ralph would have loved her more; but early care and the wearing anxieties of life had brought her spirits down to low-water mark. So sweetly uncomplaining, so watchful for Ralph's comfort, so kind and unselfish, Milly still seldom rose to the exuberance of mirth. Ralph might have doted on a gay, hoydenish, spoiled sister; but how could he be expected to know that poor Milly's back was aching, that her head grew dizzy, and her eyes weak, from too much night-work and too little sleep, when she never in the remotest way hinted at these facts?

So their evenings were generally spent in silence, the sister plying her busy needle, the brother reading, rarely aloud, as the works he perused on engineering, mechanics, and the like, full of dry terms and technicalities, were unsuited to such a purpose. It was seldom that he could spare half an hour from his studies to take up a volume of the poets or a magazine story, and weave a transient spell of romance around his sister's barren existence. With him "time was money, knowledge was power." These principles ruled and curbed all his impulses.

At ten o'clock Ralph would light his lamp, and with a curt good-night, often without a word, stalk away to his little mean bedroom. How late Milly stayed and toiled he never knew. No good-night kiss passed between them. The brother and sister were wholly undemonstrative. One never asked affection, the other never dared to offer it for fear of a repulse.

How often, when she saw that brooding, discontented look upon his face, did Milly long to go and throw her arms around his neck, to caress his cheek, to charm away the frown from his forehead, to tell him of the ardent, pure, unselfish love that filled her heart, like the waters of a never-failing spring!

O, if she only had done it, poor little Milly! who can tell but Ralph's really fine nature would have broken through its artificial crust in response to such a generous appeal? But she never did do it. Shy and sensitive, dreading a rebuff more than a physical hurt, Milly shrank farther and farther into her own shadow ; and now the humble home was broken up, the old anxious life was ended, and Ralph had parted from her without one good-bye kiss—one sign of all they had lived through and suffered in common !

Milly cried very softly behind her blue vail for twenty miles or more. The long train in its swift flight across country seemed to clank and beat out a kind of refrain to her thoughts, and the burden was ever, " I am so sorry Ralph did not kiss me good-bye."

They had startled a good many quiet country places, and rushed tumultuously over trestle-work and through tunnels, before Milly·was re-called to the present by a sudden gleam of sun-set that shot its splendors through the car win-dow. She awoke out of a fit of sad musing, to find that they had neared the banks of a pictur-esque river, and were shooting along under the shadow of some fine purple hills. The water repeated the color of these hills in a modified tone, and gently undulated through a mist of the purest violet. The sky glowed in orange tints behind ; and as it deepened, the hills and the river changed to a more unreal loveliness.

Sweeping away, like a curtain that some invisible hand had parted, rose a dark cloud, fold upon fold. Against. it floated a bit of white vapor, relieved on the dark back-ground like a stone cameo.

The thick mask of cloud and mist had parted just when the richest glow filled the heavens, and suddenly, without warning, the cone of this brightness seemed to fall apart, and scatter its dying embers along the hills, with a transient, hectic beauty that dropped down to ashes. Trees and rocks, waves and clouds, turned pallid in an instant. It was the cold, still change of death that succeeds a vision of the ineffable glories of the hereafter. There was the long-trailing cloud still, and against it that floating bit of white vapor. It appeared now to Milly's fancy, that loved to trace pictures in the clouds, like a death's head and cross-bones.

The idea brought a kind of shiver to her nerves, a half-defined, superstitious feeling of some evil to come ; but still she was fascinated, and impelled to watch the shape that seemed for many miles persistently to follow the train.

The influence of this fancy still vaguely clung about her after night had come, and she was trying to court sleep in her comfortable little berth, with the curtains drawn, and her bag and cloak stopping out the draughts.

The rumble and roar of the car seemed to retire beneath her, and sounded like innumerable trip-hammers reverberating along the rocky walls of a cavern. She could hear two men talking low in the berth next her own. One said the train shook a good deal, and it was the opinion of the other that they were running all-fired fast.

These remarks gave Milly a momentary twinge of uneasiness; but it soon passed away. She lay quite still, listening to the low, half-suppressed singing of a mother not far off, who was hushing her baby to sleep. The sound had a sort of sadness in it to the young girl's ear, and made her feel all the more the emptiness of her life and of her heart.

Now and then the car door opened, and a light gleamed for a moment along her curtain and was gone. Presently Milly fell into one of those strange states, neither sleeping nor waking. She heard distinctly the heavy breathing of the sleepers around her. She heard the stealthy tread of the conductor as he passed to and fro. But still that vision of river and sky seemed to hang before her eyes with a death's-head and cross-bones fleeting after the train. Still the rush of the engine, the clanking of the wheels, seemed to repeat in endless variations that sad, regretful under-tone of her thoughts, "I am so sorry Ralph did not kiss me good-bye!"

The scene changed as she glided more and more out toward the deep waters of oblivion. She was at home now with Ralph under the great old elms of the door-yard. They were children again; and Ralph, to tease her, was trying to climb the house. She stood below, remonstrating and pleading with clasped hands; but the rash boy had got upon the shed roof, and answered her entreaties with contemptuous words. Breathlessly she saw him cling to the angle of the main building, and then creep along the drain-pipe up, up to the ridge-pole. There he stood at last, waving down to her, until the house appeared to rise and grow so tall it touched the sky. Ralph rose with it, throwing kisses below in mockery, when his foot seemed to slip; he tottered upon the dizzy brink, wavered, strove to right himself in vain, then fell.

"My God!" A crash. Blow after blow, repeated quickly. A whirring, clashing, grinding motion; shriek upon shriek; the sharp splintering up of wood; the jagged, harsh, grating sounds from bolts and bars wrenched out of their places; the hurling down of broken, unformed masses, and there Milly lay, crushed, at the bottom of the embankment, with an indescribable weight upon her chest, that forced the blood up to her eyes and mouth—still alive, and sensible that a frightful accident had occurred.

She thought so much in the few minutes that unspeakable anguish lasted! What pen could describe those thoughts? What calm, unmoved brain could picture them? Strange to say, she thought with a kind of compassion, greater than the pity she felt for her own broken body, of that mother she had heard crooning to her baby a few hours before. Something yielding and round lay pressed against her feet. There was just sensation enough left in her toes to make that out.   Could it be the little, soft baby?   Yes, it was.

She tried to speak.   Only one articulate word came to her lips.   It was "Ralph!" and then that old emotion that had vibrated on her heart-strings so painfully ever since they parted woke even in the pit of death, with but the merest fragment of a torn and shattered mortality remaining, "O, I wish Ralph had kissed me good-bye!"   Too late for good-bye kisses; too late for atoning love; too late for reparation! The agonized dew of death was standing on Milly's forehead.   She would not have lasted long, except for a little fresh air that sifted down through a crevice of the car roof that pressed upon her bosom, and was crushed down by a mountain weight of debris.

Her right hand still retained some slight degree of feeling and motion.   She managed, with great effort, to raise it and put it through this opening.   Then she felt, so to speak, for the fingers of her left hand, but they were gone, and the whole arm with them; nothing remained in its place but a dull ache.

Presently a ray of light flashed into this

14

crevice from a lantern, and a pair of kind eyes
looked down into her filmy ones. " God! " said
the owner of the eyes, a great, stalwart man,
covered with smoke, grime, and blood, (one end
of the demolished train had taken fire, and he
had performed prodigies with his naked hands,)
as he touched Milly's little broken hand, " here
is a child. No, a young girl. Poor lamb!
poor lamb! It's the very hardest place to get
at." He stooped a little nearer, and kept the
little hand in his, chafing it softly.

" Are you a brave girl ? "

The filmy eyes looked up to his with almost
a bright, answering glance ; the little hand almost closed ; and the violet lips, with exceeding
great effort, replied, " Yes, sir." Never had
the small, plain face looked so divinely brave
and patient as it looked now.

" Glad to hear it," said the man with inspir-
ing heartiness, though his strong voice quivered
too. " Could you hold on, think, an hour, till
we pry you out ? "

" No, thank you," in a whisper. " Don't try."
The bright look changed now to a wondrous
smile.

The man bent nearer to catch the words

her lips were forming. " Would you write for me ? "

" Yes."

" Can you hear what I say ? "

" Yes."

"If you don't hear, press my hand. Ralph Fairbanks, Rexford. Dear Ralph, good-bye. God bless you ! I never told you how much I loved you. It was my fault"—her mind seemed to flicker. "Don't fret, dear ; I was to blame —only—only I'm—so sorry you didn't—kiss— me good-bye ! "

The voice came as if every word was dependent on a feebler and still feebler pulsation of the heart. At last it stopped. There was no sound to the listener's ear, only that brave, enduring look lingered upon her face. The little hand grew limp in his. He laid it reverently upon the young girl's breast, and wrenching off a piece of planking from the car roof with prodigious strength, knelt down and pressed a holy kiss on the yet warm lips.

LETTY'S RIGHTS.

———•———

ORDINARILY, little Mrs. Bennett was hopefulness itself; but she took rather a melancholy view of Letty's case, because her mind was not adapted to understand it.

"Well, mother, how goes things?" It was Ethan Bennett's question, and he used the good old-fashioned mode of address in speaking to his wife.

Ethan was a tall, stoop-shouldered farmer, well browned and seasoned by New England sun and wind, and powdered over now by the dust of travel; but Mrs. Ethan, for whom the words were meant, was rounded to just that degree of plumpness which befits a matron of her years: with the stuff dress fitting accurately over the broad, motherly bosom; with her face filling the comeliest curves; with a chin slightly double, where dimples hovered; with a nose all the better for turning up a little, and a mouth

very pleasant in spite of false teeth; and a
kindly pair of brown eyes. Now, as she stood
there on the stoop, with her dress hitching up
slightly in front, showing a neat prunella gaiter.
her face was overclouded, and she shook her
head rather dismally.

"What's to pay now, mother?" inquired
Ethan, putting down his lean carpet-satchel on
the settee.

"O, it's only Letty," groaned Mrs. Bennett.
"She's been having a fuss with the trustees, and
she says she shall leave school if they don't toe
the mark. There never was so strange a child
as Letty is. I can't make out where she gets
her sotness and her queer notions."

"It's only Letty, then," echoed Mr. Bennett,
as if Letty were a chronic difficulty in the family. "Wal, I thought for sure one of the horses
had foundered, or old Wooley been choked with
a corn-cob. I guess Letty will keep, mother,
till you get me something to eat, for I'm as
holler as a drum."

Ethan Bennett was one of those men who,
while in a state of hollowness, are utterly bereft
of ideas or inventions; so he stepped into his
own door with that infinite sense of rest which

multitudes of people never feel away from home.
His very hat, with something of the slouchy air
natural to its master, looked as if it felt better
for being hung back on the old peg.   With a
half sigh of satisfaction Ethan settled into his
favorite chair, in that corner of the sitting-room
which was handy to the file of the county paper,
and the old clock, and mother's work-table, and
afforded a glimpse of the roadway through the
parted boughs of the maple, by the gate, with
the sound of cackling hens coming from the
barn-yard.

"Mother," said Ethan, just as a chanticleer set
up a jubilant note, "there aint no roosters that
crow like ourn."

Mrs. Bennett laughed an unctuous little
laugh.   She was glad to have Ethan say such
things.   It showed that he prized his home.
She knew he was tired, though his face never
changed much ; for hadn't she, as she said, been
taking the latitude and longitude of that man
for the last twenty-five years ?   It was comfort-
ing now to look at her cheery, buxom figure as
she drew in front of him a small table, that he
might have every thing ready at a turn of his
hand, and placed thereon what, in New England

parlance, is known as a platter of cold victuals —corned beef and cabbage, potatoes, nicely pared, and rosy beets, all resting cheek by jowl on the same dish. Then she brought forth the cruet-stand, and some snowy bread, with a pat of the last churning of butter, as yellow as gold, and half a dozen long dough-nuts, twisted and twirled, and browned to perfection, crispy to the tooth and fragrant to the nostrils.

We will leave Ethan to partake of what he called his "snack," as he intended to reserve the larger portion of his appetite for the stated evening meal. It is not always an alluring sight to see a hungry man eat ; but Mrs. Ethan beamed on him delightedly. She loved, as she expressed it, "to have folks take hold hearty," especially her own husband, when he had been away on a journey. It was a substantial tribute to the comforts of home and the excellence of her cooking.

The cold victuals rapidly disappeared, and at the end of a good half hour Ethan leaned back in his chair and put his hand somewhere in the region of his stomach.

"Now, mother," said he, "what about Letty?"

"Wait till I've done this little chore," returned Mrs. Bennett, "and can take my work and sit down."

There was a basket of golden pippins on the table near at hand. Ethan took one and peeled it with his jack-knife, and let the long peel dangle lazily down. Pretty soon the wife was ready to take her place beside him, in her low chair, with the bright pieces of the patch-work she was putting together spotting the rag-car-pet, and the sunshine coming in fitfully through the branches of her window geraniums and flick-ering about her neat, homely grown. Farmers' wives are apt to grow angular and harsh of feature comparatively early ; but all the juices were preserved in good little Mrs. Bennett's composition. Ethan looked at her as if she were handsomer in his eyes now than the day they got married. Ethan was not impatient by nature. He was a slow man, and willing to bide his wife's time ; and so Letty's story was told.

"You see," she began, "that Austin has had to leave the school ; the boys hooted him out. He was a poor shack any way, if he had been to college. You can't make a whistle out of a pig's tail if you try ever so hard.

Now, the trustees have come coaxing round Letty to get her to take Austin's place for fifty dollars a quarter less than he got. But Letty says no; and you ought to see her eyes snap. She says if she does Austin's work she must have his pay; she wont take the place for a cent less. Her head is full of them new-fangled notions about woman's rights. She says women aint a-going to be put upon as they always have been. Dear, I don't know nothing how to answer her, for she can speak five words to my one; but if school breaks up and she comes home, she'll be as oneasy as a fish out of water. I shouldn't wonder if she begun to talk, just as she did last fall, about going down South to teach the colored folks. I hain't got nothing against the blacks, and I guess they're smart to learn, from all accounts; but I can't bear to have Letty streak off nobody knows where. Dear, I sometimes most wish she'd marry Sol Spinner. He's been like her shadder for a year or two. It would take the notions out of her, and I guess she'd settle down and make a stiddy woman."

"Now, mother," replied Ethan, preparing to peel his third pippin, "don't take on over Letty;

you know you're generally the one to look out
pretty sharp on the bright side. Just let Letty
alone. Give her rope. There's some women
that are like young calves—they have to have a
monstrous long tether. Letty's one o' that
kind, and this time the girl is right. I hope
she'll give old Squire Proudfut a dressing down,
for he's the ringleader among the trustees. It's
a shame to him to sit in meeting every Sunday,
under the droppings of the sanctuary, with his
face like a flint, and then go away and brow-
beat a woman. There aint a grain of justice in
Letty's not getting the same wages as a man
if she does the same work and does it as
well, and I'm glad she's going to stick to her
pint."

"Wal, maybe the child's right," said Mrs. Bennett, with a sigh that seemed ludicrous in her,
jolly and comfortable as she was—something,
in fact, like a laugh turned topsy-turvey ; " but,
for my part, I can't see where she gets her notions. I always thought the world that was
good enough for father and mother was good
enough for me. Father was a close man and
very particular. Mother had to skinch a good
deal ; so I said to myself, if I ever get married

I'll marry an easy man. And there's one thing about it, father, you are an easy man."

Ethan nodded, as if he enjoyed his reputation. "I don't know as I've got much to say against men," Mrs. Bennett went on. "I guess I've got all the rights I want. Letty says we're slaves, and she wants to vote; but I can't see much sense in it"—Ethan nodded again—"and I wish she hadn't got such notions in her head. If she'd marry Sol, she could twist him right round her little finger and he'd never know it. It's always best to let a man think he's driving even when you've got the lines in your own hands. Then there's that farm of Sol's, without a cent of incumbrance on it, and that nice stone house, that Letty could have all to herself; and such a cellar—why, there aint another like it in Huntsville."

"There's Letty, now," said Ethan, shoving up the window and letting in the mild, spicy October air, "and some of the boys are with her. School's out, sure enough."

Letty was as roundly and compactly built as her mother; but there was an energy in her little frame, and a power of command in her bonny blue eye, that held rude spirits in check.

No boy—and the Huntsville boys were a hard lot—had ever been known to ride rough-shod over Letty. Still, a gleam of fun twinkled at the corner of her mouth. She knew when and how to unbend, and play the companion with her scholars. Big and little stood by her to a boy. For a long time she had ruled the school over Mr. Austin's head, otherwise that weakling would have been hooted out at an earlier period.

As Letty opened the little gate into the front yard, the boys, with their books and slates, swarmed up on the fence.

" Let's give Miss Bennett three cheers—good, rousing fellows!" said Nate Owens, the biggest boy of all, with a flat nose, and puffy cheeks, and little twinkling black eyes. Hats and caps flew up into the air, and the cheers were given with a will.

" Boys," said Letty, facing round with dignity, " you have always behaved well toward me. Now I hope you are going to treat your new teacher, Miss Hildreth, with equal respect."

" Sho!" broke out Bob Sprowl, " Miss Hildreth! She's skim-milk watered. She haint got the spunk of a louse. We wont have any other teacher but you."

"No, no," shouted the other boys. "We'll bring old Granny Proudfoot to his oats. He needn't think he's going to put any teacher over us he pleases. Yes, sir; we are afraid of you, and we like you, too. We aint the kind of boys to get along with any teacher we aint afraid of. If we don't toe the mark, you're down on us like lightnin'; but that Miss Hildreth is mush and molasses. I guess the old school-house will be het up pretty brisk while she stays."

"You'll come back to teach us again, wont you?" piped out Billy Crofts. "Mother says I never should have got out of my abs if it hadn't been for you, for I aint quick at my spellin'."

"Go home, and be good boys," responded Letty, with a magnificent wave of the hand, though her eyes were a little damp.

The ex-school-ma'am entered the house and took off her things after kissing her father and mother.

"So you got your dander up, little gal," said Ethan, with a chuckle. "I hope you pestered old Squire Proudfut, for he's clost enough to take the hair off of a dog."

"Seems to me I'd have given in," remarked

Mrs. Bennett, " the boys all set such store by you."

"Given in!" repeated Letty, with a little melodramatic flourish. "I wouldn't take the place for any less if the whole school committee should get down on their knees to me. I don't do it for myself; I do it for my sex. Women teachers have been ground down and imposed upon long enough, and I want to show the world that there's one who wont stand it. Mother, do you understand the value of a protest."

"Lor', Letty, don't go on in that way, I don't know nothing what you mean."

"Let her talk," said Ethan. "I like to hear her. It's most as good as preachin'. She's got the hang of using big words, and I know she's in earnest when I can't understand her. Some folks think," and Ethan shook his head gravely, "that the women want to get us men folks down under foot, and keep us there, they've set up such a tarnal clatter about their rights. Let 'em, if they can. That's what I say. It's the best feller that always comes out ahead. The Lord knows I don't want to oppress women. I was always the chicken-heartedest creatur' living about 'tother sex. Mother there knows it seemed as if I should die before I could ask her to have me. I kinder blundered into it any-how. If I get my meals regular, and things are kept snug at home, then let the women vote, if they want to; but I'll be blessed if I can see why they should want to. You're right this time, Letty, and I'm glad you've stood out agin old Proudfut."

Letty, who was a singular mixture of dignity and childishness, jumped up, and put her arms round her father's neck, and gave him two hearty kisses and a hug. That evening she helped get tea and wash the dishes, although Letty disliked dish-washing. She didn't believe it was her mission in life; but she was so good and docile the little mother began to think it would be a comfort to have Letty at home after all. A day or two passed, and Letty submitted to the discipline of housework with admirable meekness. At the end of that time she packed a bag, and asked her father to take her over to Lanesburgh, on a visit to a friend.

The farm-work was slack, and Ethan had just as soon take what he called a "skoot" as not. Nothing did he like better than to jog along the country roads behind his old roan horse, Jake, with Letty by his side. Letty had an observing eye and a quick tongue, and to a slow man like Ethan supplied all his mental processes ready-made.

The school-house of Huntsville was a handsome one for a country neighborhood. It had a belfry, with a bell hung in it, and two fine class-rooms. Miss Hildreth was that morning to begin her reign ; and there was Bobby Dish, who had come a good hour before school-time, sliding down a board put through the fence, and wearing the seat of his trowsers in a manner to wring his mother's heart. As he spied Letty the lad rolled off the board, and applied a dirty little thumb to the tip of his rudimentary nose in a style which meant confusion to Miss Hildreth.

The ride to Lanesburgh was very pleasant ; for old Jake took Letty and her father through winding wood-roads, where the trees, bright with autumn tints, made sunshine in the shade, and the spiced air came softly to their senses, and the sound of dropping nuts was heard, and red squirrels were seen whisking their bushy tails over the snake-fences.

When Ethan set Letty down at her friend's (Miss Hollowell's) door she told him he need not mind about coming over after her. At the end of her visit she would take the stage as far as the Corners, which was within a mile of home. So, one afternoon, when the sun was setting in a sea of glory that seemed to fuse all things except the tree-trunks, that stood out black and bare, Letty got out of the stage and walked along the highway, with her feet making a pleasant rustle in the fallen leaves. Bob Sprowl came suddenly out of the woods, where he had been snaring birds.

"Evenin', Miss Bennett. School's all broke up in a big row. That Hildreth woman, she couldn't do nothing with the boys. We warn't agoing to let her come it over us. She had to absquatulate. And now I guess we'll have a good play-spell, unless you come back to teach us, for us boys have made a vow we wont let any body else stay."

Letty did not reprove Bob so gravely as, perhaps, she ought to have done; but she went home with a presentiment that a crisis was at hand, and that Squire Proudfoot might be obliged to eat more humble pie than he was likely to

15

relish.   Her mother was glad to find that she still remained subdued and cheerful.   Letty had what that good woman called moods and tenses; but on this particular afternoon she came in as cool and gentle as a zephyr.   Mrs. Bennett had been all day at work over the stove, putting up quinces; and she looked flushed and tired, so Letty took hold and helped get tea.   After tea there was bread to mix for next morning's baking; so she put her mother into her favorite arm-chair, and went into the buttery to sift flour, with her neat stuff dress pinned up behind over a starched petticoat, and her sleeves rolled above her dimpled elbows, and her nice little lace collar fastened with a bow of blue velvet.

She had powdered the bosom of her dress a little in dipping down into the flour-barrel, when there came a positive hard knock upon the door —such a knock as a man gives when he has a disagreeable piece of work on his hands and feels surly and out of sorts.

"Come in," called Letty; and then, as the door opened, admitting a thick-set man, muffled in a great-coat, she added, with a sparkle of malice in her bright eyes, "Good-evening, Squire

Proudfoot. Please to walk right through into the sitting-room ; you'll find father there."

The Squire stood irresolutely in the background, hemming and hawing, and thrusting out his thick knobby stick in front of him.

" Don't know as I care pertickerly about seeing your father. Thought I'd happen in and have a little chat with you."

" O, indeed ! " returned Letty, in the most ingenuous manner. " Then take a seat ; I'll be out in a minute."

She went back into the buttery and finished sifting the flour at her leisure. Letty knew the value of deliberation. When she came out her cheeks were rosy, and her little mouth looked positive and determined.

" Ahem ! Letitia," began the Squire, " what do you kalkerlate to do with yourself now you've give up school-keepin' ? "

" Farmer Lothrop offers seventy-five cents a day to any body that wants to hire out to pick up cider-apples," returned Letty, "and I think of engaging with him. It will pay better than doing a man's work and getting half his wages. Besides, it will bring up my muscle."

" 'Pears to me, Letty, you want to make yourself over into a man, don't you, though?" This was said in a peculiarly rasping tone.

"Not particularly," returned Letty, quietly.

"Now you don't say so? I've always mistrusted that you'd like to put on the trowsers."

"I should put them on if I wanted to," returned Letty, in the same manner.

"O!" ejaculated the Squire, pushing his stick out in front of him. The moment for the eating of humble pie had come, and Letty relished it keenly. There was a little awkward pause, and then the Squire said: "Wal, Letty, you've got some cur'us notions in your head; but there's one thing I will say for you—you're the best teacher we ever had in this deestrict. That Miss Hildreth dasn't say 'boo.' They kicked up an awful row. It's enough to disgrace us all over the county. The school will have to break up unless we can get you back. You see we gave Austin (here the Squire lowered his voice to a confidential point) more than we could afford. because he was one of them college-bred chaps, and there's a good deal in a name. It's enough to ruin us; but we've concluded you must have the same pay Austin had if you wont come for less. We want you to keep it hushed up, for it's setting an awful bad example ; and you see all the wimmen teachers in the neighborhood would strike for higher wages if they should find it out."

" I don't know as I want the place now," re-plied Letty, giving a vindictive screw to her rosy mouth, and kneading away industriously at the bread-making.

" O, do take it ! " urged the Squire, getting thoroughly on the anxious seat. " We sha'n't have a school worth a snap all winter unless you come back. I'd rather pay the difference out of my own pocket, if it did come pretty tough."

" Well, then," said Letty, beaming graciously upon him from her high coigne of vantage, " to oblige you, I will."

The Squire went away feeling that she had been marvelously condescending. There was somebody outside who had seen the Squire enter, and had blessed him, in a certain sense, for interfering with his own cherished plans. This young person had skulked about the yard until he caught a glimpse of Letty through the window—her dark hair and rosy face framed in a wreath of the pretty bitter-sweet vine that hung carelessly over it. He noted the snowy apron she wore, and the trim body of her dress, and the deft way she kneaded handfuls of flour into the plump mass of dough before her. Sol's heart went pit-a-pat as he opened the door; but there was no outward and visible sign that Letty's went pitty-Sol. He was a good-looking young fellow, with the fresh color an honest country life gives. There were marks of sense about his well-molded head, best expressed by the word sound; but the state of his affections at this juncture rendered him somewhat sheepish of mien. He came in and sat on the edge of the chair, holding his hat between his knees, very much as if it had contained eggs.

"Pretty warm to-night, isn't it?" said Sol, mopping his flushed face with his bandanna.

"O no!" replied Letty, keeping her back turned, provokingly enough. "I thought it was cool for the season."

"Thought I'd drop in and ask if your folks wouldn't like some of my pumpkins," quoth Sol.

"No, indeed," returned Letty. "Our barn's half full of pumpkins already."

"I wish there was something of mine you'd like to have," broke out Sol spasmodically after a painful little pause.

"I don't believe there is," returned Letty. "We raise about the same things that you do. I mean sauce."

This was too exasperating, and Sol could not endure it longer. "You know," he broke out, "that I worship the very ground you tread on."

"That's the way men talk before they get women into their power," returned Letty, kneading away at that bread as if she never intended to have done.

"'Taint talk at all," asserted Sol; "it's the living truth. Come, now, Letty, you ought to tell me whether you mean to have me or not. I can't be kept in such suspense."

"I don't mean to marry any man," returned Letty, "until I've earned some money of my own."

"You shall have all you want," cried Sol eagerly; "I'll make it over to you in black and white."

"I should only want what I earned honestly. I love independence if I am a woman," replied

Letty in a little softer tone.   "Men are stingy to their wives."

"I wouldn't be stingy to you, Letty.   I'd respect all your rights.   Come, say out square you'll have me, and I shall be the happiest fellow alive."

Sol had crept nearer and nearer in his eagerness.   Letty's hands were still engaged.   Yes, I shall have to tell it.   He was the man who dared ; he stooped and kissed Letty's cheek.

At that moment the sitting-room door opened, and Ethan surprised a situation.   "I thought I smelt fire," said he, "but I see it was only a spark."   Then he went back, and there was an explosion of laughter.

"So you and Sol have made it up between you?" said Mrs. Bennett when, a little later, Letty walked in.

"Sol was impudent," returned Letty coolly.

"He never would have been if you didn't mean to marry him," put in Ethan.

"Squire Proudfoot has come to my terms," remarked Letty, to change the subject, "and I am going back to school."

Letty taught school two years, and then she married Sol.   She kept the secret of her wages so well that at this present time there isn't a woman teacher in the vicinity whose pay doesn't equal that of a man in the same place; and accordingly Huntsville is like a city set on a hill.

THE RED EAR.

———•———

"EVERY THING must be put off until Lucy Malcom gets here. The boys are ready to break their necks for her. We mustn't let her know how much this visit has been lotted on. It will make her feel too important."

"They say there's lots of musie in Lucy," returned Uncle Dorset. Every body called him Uncle Dorset. "She's just that trim-built, light-steppin' creeter her mother was before her. What grand, good times we boys and girls used to have together when she was young! You can't have forgotten them."

"Yes," said his wife, with a slight air of injury. "You and Horace was both of you smitten with Lucy Parkes. Every body knows that well enough."

"No," replied Uncle Dorset, wagging his good-natured old head, "it was Horace's sister

I was after ; but I was always willing to crack a joke with Lucy Parkes."

"Wal," remarked Aunt Dorset, the aggrieved tone shading off a little, "it always looked as if it was nip and tuck between you and Horace."

The old lady did not really mean it ; but the truth was she had always been a little jealous of her brother's wife, and now, almost uncon- sciously, the feeling was transferred to Lucy Malcom. She did not relish the idea of her coming to Stockburn and turning people's heads, as her mother had done. She had not seen the girl for five or six years ; but report said Lucy had grown to be a pretty, arch, dark-eyed little witch, with a spice of mischief in her composition that made her quite irresist- ible. In the mild haze of the autumn day the Dorset boys were getting in the corn, drawing with an ox-team the rustling shocks to the barn—

> " The old swallow-haunted barn,
> Brown-gabled, long, and full of seams,
> Through which the moated sunlight streams."

"We will have a husking-bee when Cousin Lucy gets here," said Enoch Dorset as he stood up on the load, pitchfork in hand, his tall, well-knit form swaying a little and showing to advantage, clad as it was in a comfortable flannel shirt and trowsers of Jersey blue.

"Golly! so we will," said his brother Job from the thrashing-floor. "If Cousin Lu is as lively as they say she is, it will be general training most of the time while she stays."

Job was not as good-looking as Enoch. His hair was lank and his face was sallow ; but there were funny lines round his mouth, and he had a dry way of saying things, and a taste for drollery of all sorts, that made him a favorite. He kept his wit sharpened at Enoch's expense ; and Enoch was rather open to ridicule, for he had a sneaking fondness for hair-oil, and fancy neckties, and scented pocket-handkerchiefs, and secretly believed himself to be the best-looking fellow in Stockburn.

"Hullo!" said Enoch, standing still on the load, with that easy sway of the hips, and shading his handsome brown face with his hand as he looked up the road where it rose a little until the spiral Lombardy poplars in front of Elkanah Raynor's house showed gaps of sky between, like parted fingers, and the old chimneys nestled in a bower of fruit-trees, yellow and russet now. The road down which Enoch was gazing was by no means a common country road. The fences were all of the best, and the foot-paths were shaded by fine stocky maples, that were carpeting the wagon-track with flecks of flame color. Every house in Stockburn neighborhood was snug and neat, with a well-to-do air. It had the best school-house and church in the township, and was what people called a " crack " street.

" There's the stage coming round the turnpike corner!" exclaimed Enoch as his eyes followed a cloud of dust.

" Cousin Lucy!" shouted Job. And he threw down his fork and dashed away to the house ; and in a minute more Uncle Dorset, bare-headed, with his broad, good-natured old face smiling all over, and little bustling Aunt Dorset, with her cap-strings flying, hurried out into the front yard.

There was a face at one of the windows of the Raynor farm-house as the top-heavy stage, with its six horses, and flapping leather curtains, and piles of trunks strapped on behind, went creaking past. The house was too much shaded for health, and the face was in shadow. It was a young face, with an abundance of soft hair, regular features, and large blue eyes, that ought to have been patient and lòving; but there was an unnatural compression about the lines of the mouth that made it look a little stern. Now, as the stage passed quickly by, affording to the watching eyes at the window a glimpse of a fascinating, girlish countenance, lovely in its bloom, with a little blue vail fluttering from a jockey hat, Nancy Raynor's head bent down on her work, and it seemed as though something said in her ear, " He will love her ; I know he will love her."

So it appeared that Lucy Malcom's arrival was causing some heart-burning in Stockburn neighborhood. All unconscious of this, Lucy —the roundest, plumpest, merriest little maiden ever seen—tripped out of the stage when the driver had brought his horses to. There was a pair of sparkling black eyes adorning her rosy face, and her laugh rang out as clear as a silver bell. Lucy had various parcels, bags, and books, which she shed about as such a little minx will ; and a young man, who had got down from the stage to assist her in alighting, gathered them

up and handed them back. He was evidently
a town-bred man, with white hands, and a downward look, and too little chin, and a carefully-
kept mustache. Lucy took her things from
him in a pretty, petulant sort of a way, giving
him a curt little bow; and the next moment
they were all on the ground, and she had her
arms hugged tightly round Uncle Dorset's
neck.

"Don't you mean to give me one of them,
Cousin Lucy?" inquired Enoch, leaning, in one
of his naturally graceful postures, against the
gate as the kisses went flying about. "I think
I ought to come in for my share."

The saucy little maiden shook her black
tresses very decidedly, making eyes at Enoch,
Aunt Dorset thought, just as Lucy Parkes used
to do; and the next moment, in one of her
capricious fits, she embraced old Job with her
chubby little arms and gave him a sounding
smack. From that time her flirtation with
Enoch may be said to have begun.

"Who is that spruce-looking young fellow
who helped you out of the stage, Lucy?" inquired Aunt Dorset, gazing through her honest
old specs. "Is he an acquaintance of yours?"

The young man had mounted to the driver's seat while the operation of getting the trunk off was in progress, and appeared to be watching the group in the door-yard under the locust-trees with considerable interest.

"O, I believe he has got business somewhere around here," returned Lucy, with an indifferent toss of her head. "He was very civil to me on the journey."

"I am afraid you are a bit of a flirt, child," said Aunt Dorset. And then she thought to herself, "Her mother was before her; pity if she shouldn't be."

"Me a flirt! O, auntie!" and Lucy's black eyes rolled up, and her mouth puckered itself into a dewy, rosy exclamation point.

They were in the house now, and Aunt Dorset had shown her niece up to the best room, shut up as best rooms are apt to be in the country, and rather heavy with old mahogany furniture, and a high-post bedstead, with its dimity-teaster and mountain of feathers. The moment the little dumpling of an old lady had trotted out of the room to fetch something that had been forgotten, Lucy skipped to the window, pushed back the blinds, and let her handkerchief flutter out in the breeze. Strange to say, there was an answering signal from the top of the stage. Enoch, who was lingering below in the yard, saw the maneuver, and said to himself, " She's a regular little case. I believe she knows more about that fellow than she pretends."

Lucy had been brought up in a town of considerable size, where French fashions prevailed ; and she had brought all her little gauds and furbelows to Stockburn, with the hope of electrifying the natives, for her soul was by no means above such feminine triumphs. She opened her trunk, and hung some trinkets about her plump little person, and nestled some bows of cherry ribbon among her glossy black curls. She went down stairs just before tea.

"How nice it is here!" said Lucy, looking out through the sitting-room window at the sunny old garden. "I have always been cooped up in a town, Uncle Dorset, and now you must teach me to be a country girl."

" I s'pose you think, don't you," inquired the old gentleman, " that some cows give buttermilk, just as Dr. Hillyer's niece did when she came up here on a visit from York ? "

16

"Perhaps I do," returned Lucy, archly, bursting into a merry laugh; "and then, you know, I solemnly believe that potatoes grow on bushes."

"Do see Lucy snuggled up to your father, and he looks as pleased as cuffy," said Aunt Dorset to Job as she put a drawing of tea in the pot. "There's a good deal of the cat about that girl. The Parkeses have all got it, every one of them."

"I wouldn't mind having her purr round me," responded Job in his dry way.

They were seated at the pleasant tea-table now. Enoch had come in, and Lucy was the center of every body's attentions. In spite of Lord Byron's churlish opinion, she was perfectly charming while engaged with her knife and fork.

"Tell me, Enoch," inquired she, "are there any nice girls in this neighborhood? I don't care a fig for young men, (there was a sly twinkle in her eye,)—they are horrid, conceited creatures; but I should like to get acquainted with a nice girl."

"Nancy Raynor is our next neighbor's daughter," said Uncle Dorset, "and she is as likely a girl as ever was raised here in Stockburn."

"She has got what I call pretty manners," put in Aunt Dorset, dishing out the stewed quinces. "Most of the girls nowadays are too brazen to suit my old-fashioned notions."

"Ask Enoch about her," said Job, with a droll wink.

"O, yes," struck in Uncle Dorset, "Enoch and Nancy used to be very thick; and I can't say whether it's her fault or his'n that they don't hitch horses any more."

Enoch colored as he bent over his plate, and Lucy cast a mischievous little glance at him.

"Nancy don't come here near as often as she used to," said Aunt Dorset, pouring out the old gentleman's second cup of tea, and putting in what he called a "long sweetening." "She aint the kind of girl to let any young man think she's going to break her heart about him. She's an independent little piece, if she does look as if butter wouldn't melt in her mouth. All the Raynors are hard-bitted."

Enoch looked really annoyed now, and kept his eyes fixed on his plate, to avoid Lucy's wicked little glances.

Suddenly he looked up, and said to her: "If you get acquainted with Nancy you can wave your pocket-handkerchief out of the window. I believe you like that sort of thing." Now it was Lucy's turn to cast down her eyes.

The house was full of fun and music, just as Uncle Dorset had predicted. Lucy kept things pretty well stirred up, and plotted against Aunt Dorset's steady, jog-trot, old-fashioned ideas. She wanted to have her finger in every body's pie. She meddled with the cooking, and made little mortified-looking cakes, that nobody could eat.

"'Pears to me these biscuits have got the measles," said Uncle Dorset one morning as he broke one open, decorated with a number of yellow eyes.

"I made them, dear," said Lucy, looking so penitent. "You know I've been brought up in dreadful ignorance; but now I am learning to cook, for I expect to marry a poor man—perhaps a farmer." And she cast such a glance at Enoch that Aunt Dorset took the alarm. That same afternoon, while Enoch was down in the Evans lot, mending a piece of fence, to keep Squire Bridgam's cattle out, his anxious mother appeared, with her apron over her head.

"Look here, Enoch," said she, "the neighbors have got it round that you are going to make a match with Lucy Malcom. I wouldn't be quite so pertickerler toward her if I was you. It never turns out well for first cousins to marry."

"The neighbors may just mind their own business," said Enoch, angrily, as he hammered away at a board.

"Tut, tut," returned his mother, who had a temper of her own. "It takes a flirt to catch a flirt, and I shouldn't wonder if you and Lucy were well matched. To speak plain, I don't think you have treated Nancy Raynor right; and the day may come when you will find out what a true heart is worth."

In spite of all this Aunt Dorset liked the creature. Lucy compelled liking from those who did not wholly approve of her. She was disorderly and upsetting, and shocked the old lady's ideas of method and regularity; but still she would bear more from her than from any body else. Job liked Lucy's spirit of fun. She

was not too big to play tom-boy, and to follow
the boys into the field and ride home on a load
of pumpkins, looking like a little queen amid
her golden treasures. She had seen Nancy
Raynor in the singers' seat at church of a Sunday morning, but that was as near as the two
girls had approached each other. In response
to Lucy's teasing, Aunt Dorset had invited the
neighbor's daughter to tea; but on the afternoon of the day appointed Nancy had sent to
say that she must be excused on account of a
bad headache. Job comforted Lucy by saying
that Nancy would surely come to the husking-
bee; but Nancy, as she lay awake nights, with
the tears wetting her cheeks, thought to herself that she would not go and witness that
girl's triumph. From her place of vantage
by the window, with her face looking pale
and her breath coming fast, she had watched
Enoch pass by in the moonlight, with Lucy
clasping his arm and gazing up in his face,
and she almost despised herself because she
could not see it unmoved.

Enoch was bewitched by Lucy, but the bewitching did not go very far. He was a young
man who had a very good opinion of himself,

and his constancy had not been developed. He liked to have a number of girls fond of him, and he thought it was rather a fine thing to cool off toward a flame, as he had done toward Nancy Raynor. Still, with all her innocent, pussy-like ways, Enoch distrusted Lucy. He had caught her sending billets privately to Middletown by the farm-hand, Zeke, and he had not forgotten her adventure in the stage-coach.

The preparations for the husking-bee were almost complete, and Lucy was quite wild with delight. The big barn was to be nicely illuminated, and the supper of pumpkin-pie, dough-nuts, and cider to be spread in the kitchen in the good old orthodox fashion. Afterward the great barn-floor was to be cleared, and black fiddlers, engaged at Middletown, were to play for dancing.

Two days before the husking-bee was to come off, Lucy made Job an apple-pie bed. Job meant to be even with her, and the next afternoon he called up the stairway:

"Cousin Lucy, don't you want to take a ride behind Brown Betty?"

Lucy was, of course, delighted with the propositiou, so she stepped to the window and peeped through the blinds, and there was Brown Betty hitched to the sulky—a light, airy thing, that looked as if made of cobwebs, with the tiniest of backless seats hung in the middle. Lucy appreciated the joke, and, while Job ran back to the carriage-house to get his coat, she slipped down stairs, unhitched Brown Betty, and was. off down the road like a flash.

"O, massy to. us!" screeched Aunt Dorset, running to the door. "That child will surely get killed. She don't know nothing about driving, and the mare is as skittish as a colt."

Job dashed out of the carriage-house, looking crestfallen enough. "She's a plucky little piece of baggage," said he, "and there's no use trying to get ahead of her. Don't worry, mother; Lucy is able to take care of herself."

There certainly was a sweet little cherub somewhere up aloft, who looked out for audacious Lucy. In an hour's time she came back, with a demurely wicked gleam in her eye. Brown Betty had evidently been put through her paces. Lucy threw down the lines with a professional air, and ordered Job to give her nag

Lucy's Ride with Brown Betty.

"O m'assy to us," screeched Aunt Dorset, "that child will surely get killed."

some water, "for she is as dry as a contribution-box," she added; "and I would like to know who is a little sulky now."

Lucy explained, later, that accidentally she had met Mr. Allen, the young man who was polite to her in the stage. In return for turning her horse around, she had asked him to come over to the husking-bee.

The night of the husking-bee had come, and Milton Raynor was blacking his boots at the back-door of the farm-house.

"Aren't you going over to Dorset's to-night?" he inquired of his sister.

"No, I am not."

"Now I would, if I was you, Nancy. It don't look well for you to stay cooped up here at home. Folks will begin to say you are love-sick."

"I don't care what they say," returned Nancy, and her voice sounded harsh and metallic in her own ears. She went up to her room, and sat down by the little window, that was festooned by the Virginia creeper, burning with a deep autumnal crimson. The moonlight was falling still and white on the stubble-fields and belts of woods. It blanched Nancy's face—not a patient or submissive face. Her eyes might have read a poem in that lovely evening, but they were full of trouble. She wanted to crush out the core of constancy and devotion in her heart, but she knew not how to do it. She was too restless to stay within doors, so she wrapped her head and shoulders in a shawl, and glided out into the shadow of the trees along the roadside, until she came nearly opposite to Uncle Dorset's house, where she could see the lights from the barn and catch the sounds of fun and frolic from the huskers. She was haunted by an irrational desire to spy upon Enoch and Lucy, and to confirm what she so much dreaded to find true.

Mr. Allen arrived early, and with his white hands, his want of chin, black mustache, and city-made clothes, quite captivated the rustic beauties of Stockburn. But Nelly Blake, a blue-eyed little blonde, received a much larger share of his attention than Lucy Malcom did ; although Lucy, in her scarlet spencer and black skirt, below which peeped the trimmest of ankles and tidiest of buskin shoes, was certainly very charming. She was always with Enoch, laughing and sparring and flinging about her bright, saucy wit. Enoch had just whispered to her that if he found the red ear she would have to suffer, when some one screamed that Mr. Allen had found it. The dove-cote was ruffled, and the girls scampered over the piles of corn and hid in the horse-stalls, trying to avoid the penalty of a kiss. At last the young man took after Lucy, and the light-footed little minx gave him a chase round the barn, and then dashed away through the door into the moonlight, he after her, and the ring of her silver laugh was the last that was heard of little Lucy.

In the confusion nobody missed them. The whole company went to supper pretty soon, and more than half an hour had passed when Enoch came and took hold of Job's coatsleeve. They stepped outside the kitchen-door together, and then Enoch said, in an agitated whisper:

"For Heaven's sake, where is Cousin Lucy? That fellow Allen has disappeared too. Can it be she is playing one of her pranks? Father has gone to bed. Don't speak to mother yet. Get a light and come up to her room with me."

The two brothers slipped noiselessly up the staircase into Lucy's chamber, where the moonlight was lying quietly upon the carpet. Everything seemed just as usual, only a note lay on the bureau, addressed to Uncle Dorset, in Lucy's pretty girlish handwriting. Enoch snatched it and tore it open. It ran as follows :

"Don't be cross and scold me, that's a dear. I am going to marry Charley Farnsworth. He isn't Mr. Allen at all. I think pa has been very cruel toward Charley. He wouldn't let him come to the house, because he was a little wild once. But now Charley has reformed, and don't drink a drop ; and if he couldn't get into business, I am sure it wasn't his fault, poor fellow. The only business he had in Middletown was seeing me. Maybe you will think I am to blame ; but I do love Charley to distraction, and we mean to get married this very night. Nobody need follow us, for it will be too late."

Perhaps Enoch uttered an oath ; at any rate, he crushed the note in his hand. "Go down stairs, Job," said he, "and try and keep the folks agoing. Get up a game if you can. Don't tell mother quite yet. I will put Zeke on one of the farm-horses and mount Brown Betty myself; and perhaps we can bring the crazy girl to her senses. The fellow looked to me like a sneak, and I dare say he is after Uncle Horace's money. Wont the old gentleman fume, though."

Enoch ten minutes later was spurring along the moon-lit road, when he caught sight of a fluttering garment among the trees by the way.

"Who is there," he called out sharply. As no answer came, he alighted, took the bridle over his arm, and pushed into the shadows.

"It's me, Nancy Raynor," said a faint voice.

"You, Nancy, out alone this time of night! Did you see any body pass here half an hour back?" he asked, hurriedly. "I am afraid my cousin, Lucy Malcom, has made a fool of herself, and gone off with a scamp who has been hanging round here ever since she came."

Nancy had often thought in just what scornful tones she would speak to Enoch Dorset if he ever chanced to be humiliated in her presence; but now the opportunity had come, and all her vindictiveness had vanished.

"And do you care so very much about her?" she asked in a faltering voice.

"I don't care in the way you think I do' Nancy," and Enoch's better nature suddenly asserted itself. "The only girl I ever really cared for was you, and I was a fool and a coxcomb. I thought I could play with you; and when I wanted to come back, you were like ice toward me. Of course, I deserved it. I deserve that you should punish me, perhaps should never speak to me again."

"O, Enoch! How miserable I have been," sobbed Nancy as her head went down. Enoch found a moment in which to comfort her before he leaped again on his horse and darted away after the fugitives. But they were not found that night. The next day Lucy came, with her graceless husband, and threw herself at Uncle Dorset's feet, and begged him to intercede with her father. He could not help promising any thing while Lucy had her arms around his neck, and so he did intercede, and the old man relented in a few months, and Lucy was taken back into favor. The little cherub that sits up aloft has never deserted her, and Charley has turned out better than could have been expected. He takes care of the babies, and is good to his flyaway wife, and makes jokes of how he won her with the red ear in that old husking-bee.

When Nancy married Enoch folks said she was too good for him. And so she was; but she has helped to make a man of him, and Enoch would be ready to chastise any body who should even hint that he does not love his wife dearly.

THE END.

CPSIA information can be obtained
at www.ICGtesting.com
Printed in the USA
BVHW04*1029081018
529578BV00010B/158/P